# The House Built From Beyond

When Sarah Pardee Winchester's husband died, he left her with two things: the fortune he made from his repeating rifles and the guilt from its victims. To ease her mind, Sarah sought to accommodate those unfortunate souls. Through séances, she asked the spirits to design a dwelling place for them on earth. The result is a macabre 148-room hotel for the undead, the Winchester House in San José, California. Haunted to this day, you may find yourself there—be it in this life or the next.

# 55 M.P.H. Dark Zone

If you're traveling north on New Jersey's Garden State Parkway, don't be surprised if you're flagged down by an accident victim who doesn't exist. For over thirty years, the Parkway Phantom has been jump-starting the hearts of many weary late-night travelers. Though there is no official explanation for him, the Phantom regularly lurches out in front of traffic near Exit 82 several times a year. So the next time you're in Jersey, buckle up and beware—the life you save may be your own.

\* \* \*

Inside you'll find
these unnerving
a *dark zone* that

D1563841

## ALSO BY THE AUTHOR

True Tales of the Unknown
True Tales of the Unknown: The Uninvited
True Tales of the Unknown: Beyond Reality
Dead Zones*

*Published by
WARNER BOOKS

**ATTENTION: SCHOOLS AND CORPORATIONS**

WARNER books are available at quantity discounts with bulk
purchase for educational, business, or sales promotional use. For
information, please write to: SPECIAL SALES DEPARTMENT,
WARNER BOOKS, 1271 AVENUE OF THE AMERICAS, NEW
YORK, N.Y. 10020.

**ARE THERE WARNER BOOKS
YOU WANT BUT CANNOT FIND IN YOUR LOCAL STORES?**

You can get any WARNER BOOKS title in print. Simply send title
and retail price, plus 50¢ per order and 50¢ per copy to cover
mailing and handling costs for each book desired. New York State
and California residents add applicable sales tax. Enclose check
or money order only, no cash please, to: WARNER BOOKS, P.O.
BOX 690, NEW YORK, N.Y. 10019.

# DARK ZONES

## EDITED BY SHARON JARVIS

**WARNER BOOKS**

A Time Warner Company

If you purchase this book without a cover you should be aware that this book may have been stolen property and reported as "unsold and destroyed" to the publisher. In such case neither the author nor the publisher has received any payment for this "stripped book."

WARNER BOOKS EDITION

Copyright © 1992 by Sharon Jarvis
All rights reserved.

Cover Design by Diane Luger
Cover Photograph by Craig Aurness/Westlight

Warner Books, Inc.
1271 Avenue of the Americas
New York, N.Y. 10020

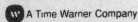 A Time Warner Company

Printed in the United States of America

First Printing: August, 1992

10  9  8  7  6  5  4  3  2  1

# CONTENTS

# ACKNOWLEDGMENTS

Without the contributions of the following people, this book would not be possible:

Margaret L. Carter, Joel Martin, Chris Martin, Elyse Martin, Dr. L. Stafford Betty, Gene Snyder, Roberta Klein-Mendelson, Bruce G. Hallenbeck, Ulrich Magin, John Brizzolara, Michael Hammonds, Dan Valkos, Norman Basile, Rich Rainey, Bradley Sinor, D. Douglas Graham, Gail Larson Toerpe, Nancy A. Cucci, Mary Ann Bramstrup, Lee Svensson, Thom Sciacca, Susan B. Fensten, Scott Green, Patrick A. McCurdy, Maurice Schwalm, Cliff Crook, Mary Ellen Meredith, and Norm Gauthier.

Thanks to Sam McDonald of the *Danville Register and Bee* and to the Curator of Manuscripts, University Archivist, University of Virginia Library, Charlottesville, VA 22901, for source material for "The Talking Cat of Danville."

A very detailed account of Dr. L. Stafford Betty's Kern City, California, investigation appeared in a 1984 journal published by the Society For Psychical Research, 1 Adam and Eve Mews, London W8 6UG, England. Another version appeared in the September and October 1987 issues of *Fate* magazine.

Thanks to Terry Vellar of Pueblo's Oxford Bar and Grill for his assistance.

If you have questions or comments, or information about a Dead (or Dark) Zone in your area, please contact the nearest researcher:

Sharon Jarvis
RR2, Box 16B
Laceyville, PA 18623

Ulrich Magin
Stuhlbruderhofstr. 4
W-6704 Mutterstadt
Germany

Rich Rainey
(upstate New York)
c/o Sharon Jarvis at
the above address

Roberta Klein-
Mendelson
Psychic Consultant
P.O. Box 94
Monsey, NY 10952-
0094

Gene Snyder
Literature Team
Brookdale Community
College
Brookdale, NJ 07738

Bruce G. Hallenbeck
P.O. Box 753
Valatie, NY 12184

Patrick McCurdy
P.O. Box 52
Summit, NJ 07901

Joel Martin
P.O. Box 5442
Babylon, NY 11707

Maurice Schwalm
P.O. Box 3522
Kansas City, MO
66103-0522

D. Douglas Graham
P.O. Box 1148
Ballwin, MO 63022

Dan Valkos
RR #16, Comp. 39
Thunder Bay, Ontario
P7B 6B3 Canada

Norm Gauthier
P.O. Box 142
Manchester, NH 03105

Cliff Crook
Bigfoot Central
P.O. Box 147
Bothell, WA 98041-0147
1-800-83-BIGFOOT;
locally 483-4007

Bradley Sinor
1127 N. Juniper Avenue
Broken Arrow, OK
74012

When contacting contributors to this book, please
enclose a self-addressed stamped envelope. For
Canada or overseas addresses, enclose an
international postal coupon.

*We Are Not Forgotten* by George Anderson and
Joel Martin is available from Berkeley Books.

# AUTHOR'S NOTE

Unless specified otherwise, all places and names
are real.

# INTRODUCTION

For all of my life, I've always been interested in strange things. I wasn't strange personally, mind you, just fascinated by the offbeat. I loved to read ghost stories and watch horror movies and pretend that a UFO was just over the horizon. Good, clean childish fun.

Yet by the time I was a teenager, I had a poltergeist (noisy ghost) in my bedroom, which no one but me heard. And my mother had been startled by a Saturday morning phone call from the Long John Nebel television show—a show devoted to the occult and UFOs—making sure the letter they'd received from me really came from a kid.

Over the years, more bizarre things happened. And although I'd read a lot of books about weird stuff, when the weird stuff actually happened to *me*, I was just like everybody else in this world: I'd ignore it. It couldn't be real.

It took a long time for me to understand and accept that there are energies, forces, spirits—call them what you will—in the next world which cross over into this world. I call these places Dead Zones and Dark Zones. They *are* real. The stories in this book are based on actual people, genuine events, documented investigations, and firsthand accounts of witnesses. They have been supplied by such people as investigative reporters, psychics, occult researchers, and scientists.

We all welcome you to join us in the Dark Zones, where our world ends and the next one begins. . . .

Sharon Jarvis

# The Wraiths
# of Whaley House

I n the early 1850s, "Yankee Jim" Robinson was a sailor
who jumped ship, the schooner *Plutus*, while it was anchored in San Diego Bay, California. He stole a pilot
boat and, instead of fleeing, went sightseeing. Since people
depended on the water for much of their transportation, the
theft of the boat was considered a serious offense and Robinson was soon arrested.

When he struggled to free his arms from the tight ropes
binding him, a member of the posse struck him on the head
with a rusty saber. While in jail, Robinson developed a high
fever from the wound, rendering him unconscious for most
of his trial. He was awake, though, when the drunken judge
sentenced him to hang.

So, on a September night in 1855, a dazed and stunned
Robinson stood under the gallows atop a buckboard pulled
by a team of mules. The hangman's noose was tied to a crude
crossbar erected by the U.S. Army earlier in the year during
the Indian uprising. The scaffolding proved to be too short—
Yankee Jim was a big six feet four inches—and the poor man

dropped a mere five feet. Instead of dying instantly, he slowly strangled for forty-five minutes. His body was consigned to an unmarked grave.

One member of the crowd watching Robinson's execution was an Irishman from an old Brooklyn family who'd come to California in search of gold. Five years later, Thomas Whaley paid $1.50 for the same plot of land where Robinson died.

Begun in 1856 and completed a year later, the Whaley House was built on the very spot of the execution. The mansion was built by Whaley for his intended bride Anna. Where the gallows once stood is now an archway dividing the music room from the front parlor. It is known as the "haunted arch" because people have seen a shadowy figure lurking there and the spot feels extremely cold.

A few years after the mansion was built, local officials leased the granary portion of it for use as a courthouse. They requested expensive modifications of the building; Whaley complied and so the house was used as a public courtroom from 1869 to 1871. During that time, Whaley continually tried to collect for the cost of the alterations to the house, but the officials refused.

As a protest, Whaley held the county's furniture and court records hostage. The town threatened to shoot him but instead got a court order demanding the return of the county property. Whaley ignored them, and since no attempt was made to enforce the order, he left on a brief business trip. While he was gone, town officials staged a midnight raid, held his wife Anna at gunpoint, and took back their property.

Whaley spent the rest of his life writing furious letters to the county board. His demands for back rent and reimbursement for damages inflicted by the raiding party were ignored. He died in 1890, Anna in 1913. The last of their children lived in the house and died in 1953. Thomas Whaley's demands remained unresolved, but in 1956 partial atonement was made when the county, at the urging of the historical society, bought the dilapidated house to restore as a historic landmark.

But Thomas Whaley remains dissatisfied: Numerous visitors to the house have seen the ghost of a very angry man resembling Whaley. His stomping can also be heard in the old courtroom. Tourists today, moving through the house in groups, report the smell of cigar smoke—Whaley's favorite Havanas.

Along with Whaley is his wife Anna. Visitors smell her distinctive perfume, and they often exclaim about the wonderful cooking smells—especially the baked apples—coming from the long-defunct kitchen.

And the two ghosts probably have Yankee Jim for company. Visitors and staff members hear footsteps walking across the second floor, from the sitting room to the top of the stairs—exactly over the spot where Yankee Jim was hanged.

There are other spirits as well. One is said to be that of a neighbor child named Washburn, a playmate of the Whaley children. One day, while running to join her friends in the backyard, she struck a low-hanging clothesline and died of her injuries as Mr. Whaley carried her into the kitchen. The girl's spirit has been seen but, oddly enough, only by other children who have no way of knowing who she is.

Keeping the phantom host company is the Whaley family dog, Dolly. The dog is seen by staff and visitors alike, although no animals are allowed in the building at any time. People have heard invisible horses at the front gate, a man laughing, a crying baby, the pounding of a judge's gavel, and organ music. Occasionally heavy perfume fills the air or cigar smoke fills a room, but the smoke alarms never go off.

Witnesses have seen a bedspread, a chandelier, a rocking chair, and a row of kitchen utensils move by themselves. In the courtroom, chains that separate the magistrate's area from the rest of the room sway by themselves. Windows spontaneously open, setting off the burglar alarms.

One visitor in the courtroom saw the apparition of a small, dark woman in a calico dress. In 1963, a ghostly group of men in frock coats were seen carrying on a lively discussion in the study.

Several psychics have investigated Whaley House. In 1965, famous medium Sybil Leek held a séance there, hosted by Regis Philbin and his television camera crew. Leek was contacted by a male spirit who demanded reparation for injustices committed against him—obviously Thomas Whaley. Parts of the taped séance included complaints which matched word for word some of the letters written by Whaley and which had never been made public. Leek was also contacted by another male spirit who was ill with a fever and begged for water. Was this the ghost of Yankee Jim?

In 1968, Kay Sterner, founder and president of the California Parapsychology Foundation, was approached by the then director, June Reading, about the house. The director felt the house appeared to be haunted or possibly was the site of poltergeist activity: Ghostly footsteps had been heard in the master bedroom and on the stairs. Bolted windows would open by themselves, all hours of the night and day. When fastened down with three 4-inch bolts on each side, the windows still opened, automatically setting off the burglar alarm.

Sterner, a sensitive and clairvoyant, visited the house twice, accompanied by various people who recorded her impressions. On the first visit she did not enter the house but walked around the grounds, since it was sunset and the house was closed. As she rounded the southern side, she had a vision of a man hanging from a primitive scaffolding, a team of mules just pulling away from it. . . .

Sterner continued around the house and happened to look

up. She saw a gaudily dressed woman with a painted face leaning out of a second-story window. (Later June Reading confirmed that in November 1868 the second floor had been leased out to a theatrical group.) When she reached the northern wing of the house, Sterner suddenly felt freezing cold. The director later told her that at one time a mortuary stood on that spot.

On Easter Sunday 1968, Sterner made her second visit. This time she spent part of the night there, sitting alone in the dark in an upstairs hallway. She saw the specter of an attractive young woman coming toward her. The woman wore a well-tailored gown of an odd brown color. Her straight, dark brown hair was worn simply, pinned back and allowed to fall past her shoulders. In the woman's hand was an old-fashioned razor with a bone handle. In the other was a leather razor strop. She calmly wrapped the leather around her neck. Then she picked up and ate something which she called a bitter herb. Sterner recognized it as poisonous. All in all, Kay had the impression that the young woman had tried to kill herself a total of three times.

But these visions were followed by another of the young woman with a man. He grabbed the woman by the throat as if to keep her quiet about something. June Reading informed Sterner that a young woman named Sara—matching Sterner's description—once lived in the house. She tried to kill herself with a razor. Later she was supposed to have shot herself, but the gun was never found. Sterner felt that Sara was disturbed about something, but did not kill herself—she was murdered, possibly by the man Sterner saw.

In another vision, Sterner heard loud agonizing screams as she witnessed the reenactment of a violent crime. A Mexican man and woman were quarreling; he accused her of being unfaithful, pulled out a knife, and slashed her deeply. Once again, Reading confirmed a similar historical account. At one time a Mexican couple were tenants and that the husband had murdered his wife in a bitter quarrel.

Sterner also sensed the death of a child in the "borning room" (the rear study). Again, Reading corroborated her vision with an historical account.

In trying to pinpoint why the Whaley House was the site of so much spectral phenomena, Sterner said the house was the "focal point of seismographic energy." She felt that there was an accumulation of gases and water under the subsoil that was under pressure. Although she did not know it, at one time the waters of San Diego Bay came very close to the house. Later, engineers diverted the channel, but there was still much underground water.

As further proof of her theory, Sterner pointed out that in the nearby Spanish cemetery, the Campo Santo, every time there was a burial, a phosphorescent light was seen. Mexicans were afraid to pass the cemetery at night after a funeral, thinking this light was a restless spirit. Sterner thought that instead it might be marsh gas—a strange theory for a clairvoyant who is used to seeing ghosts.

Marsh gas, metaphysical malarkey, or genuinely agitated ghosts? Keep in mind that world-famous ghost hunter Hans Holzer, deeply impressed by the manifestations in the Whaley House, called it "probably one of the most actively haunted mansions" in existence.

And the Whaley House has been officially designated by the U.S. Department of Commerce as haunted!

Whaley House is in the Old Town section of San Diego, located at the corners of San Diego Avenue and Harney Street. Take Interstate Highway 8 and get off at the Taylor Street exit. Turn left onto Juan Street and go three blocks to Twiggs Street, where free parking is available. Walk one block west to San Diego Avenue; the Whaley house is on the next corner. Telephone 619–298–2482 for further information.

# The Spirit Express

"**P**eople were scared," said Bruce Hallenbeck's grandmother.

Bruce's grandmother, eighty-five years old but still sharp as a tack, recalled the incident that happened fifty years ago in Chatham, New York.

"They were worried and upset," she said, "when the train came through—because it wasn't a real train.

"Everyone was talking about it. They were all perplexed at such a thing. It looked like any train, but it made no noise. It just went on through town without stopping."

And why were they frightened? Because no one could imagine such a thing—and yet it happened.

Fifty years ago, people may have been talking about the ghost train, but most Chatham residents today either don't know about the ghost train . . . or simply won't discuss it.

Bruce G. Hallenbeck is a paranormal investigator, especially interested in stories about his own backyard (upstate New York). And so he was intrigued with his grandmother's tale of the ghost train of Chatham. A search through the records of the town newspaper, the *Chatham Courier*, failed to turn up any stories. And yet old-timers insist they remember it. The train was also written about in a 1978 book called *Weird America* by Jim Brandon.

Chatham (formerly called Groat's Corners) is bisected by a railroad track. It may be best known as the home of the Three Stooges. Yes, Moe, Shemp, and Curly Howard all grew up on a nearby farm. Yet the entire region is rife with ghostly happenings (though, as far as we know, there have been no reports of Stoogelike ghosts).

Old-timers say there is not one ghost train but *two*! Supposedly the trains are two ancient, antiquated steam trains that occasionally make their way through town—usually on a night in late April.

The black engines have broad smokestacks and are brass-encrusted. The rolling stock is shrouded in black crepe, which flutters in the wind. No firemen or engineers can be seen. The first train has a few flatcars, and on one sits a very large band. Although the band members are playing their instruments, no sound can be heard. The second train has only one flatcar, which carries a solitary coffin.

The entire ghostly procession passes by in unearthly silence. Supposedly time stands still while the train passes, because the next "real" trains pull into Chatham five to eight minutes late.

According to some, this apparition may be Abraham Lincoln's funeral train, which passed by Chatham in April 1865 on its way back to Illinois, his birthplace. Although it is not an exact match to the description of the real Lincoln procession, this is the way some people in the area have described it.

Jack Donohue, a Chatham resident until his death in 1988, worked as a janitor at Chatham High School. Sometimes he would walk home fairly late at night. One night, in late April 1978, he saw something that few are privileged to see.

"It was an old steam train," he told Bruce Hallenbeck. "But the hell of it was that it didn't make a sound. It just sort of glided through the middle of town. The streets were deserted, so I don't imagine anybody else saw it. They certainly didn't hear it."

The train passed through town and disappeared into the darkness. "I didn't see any engineer or anybody else on the train," said Jack, "although I thought there might have been a shadow of somebody sitting at a window on one of the cars.

"I don't necessarily think it was a funeral train," Jack continued, "but it looked like it was black. And there were curtains at the windows . . . blue curtains. I've always wondered where that train came from or where it went. Maybe it takes dead souls to heaven."

Perhaps Jack Donohue had a point. Could the phantom train be the Spirit Express? All aboard, no stops until you get to the Pearly Gates? If that's the case, then by now Mr. Donohue has traveled that line himself and has long since reached his destination.

# Haunts of the Bayview Hotel

T he idea of doing a television program on ghosts and haunted houses had been on producer/director Jerry MacDermid's mind for some time. Chance (if there really is such a thing) brought him together with psychic Dan Valkos. Valkos had just finished doing an hour-long interview, which inspired Jerry MacDermid's associate to come to Valkos for a private reading. She wanted to find out more information about her immediate future and, since Valkos is a professional clairvoyant, he was able to help her out.

After the session, she mentioned to Valkos that MacDermid was thinking about doing a show about supernatural goings-on in the Sault Ste. Marie area of Ontario. She asked Valkos if he had any television experience and if he would be interested. Valkos said yes to both questions and a meeting was arranged for later that evening.

MacDermid and Valkos hit it off right away, almost as though they'd been old friends (Valkos found out later that there were past-life ties between the two of them). The two of them made room in their busy schedules and a tentative shooting date was set for late March 1988.

Since Valkos was not familiar with the Sault Ste. Marie area of Ontario, it became the television crew's job to find, in fact or in fantasy, haunted houses. The crew also searched for individuals who believed they had seen a ghost. Once this information had been gathered, Valkos's job was to host the show, narrate it, and generally be the interviewer and "ghost hunter."

Jerry MacDermid did some publicity about his forthcoming show and was contacted by a number of people claiming to have haunted houses. Soon word was received that the crew had set up an itinerary and Valkos and MacDermid were to join them in Sault Ste. Marie. However, when the time came for the two men to leave, there was a problem. As the plane prepared to leave the Thunder Bay airport, the pilot announced that Sault Ste. Marie was blanketed by heavy fog. There was a good chance the plane would have to be diverted to North Bay or Dusbury.

The two men were disturbed because they were on a rather tight shooting schedule and any delay would be sure to cause major problems. Since there were only three passengers on the plane, the pilot took a vote. He asked them if they wanted to chance it or wait for a much later flight in hopes of the fog lifting.

Instinct told Valkos that they would land on time, so he told the pilot that they would be fine and to take off. The plane left Thunder Bay and, about twenty minutes before they landed, the fog lifted! Almost immediately after they were ground, the fog returned and settled back around the airport.

MacDermid asked Valkos if he had anything to do with the fog lifting. Valkos just smiled at him.

Once they landed, they joined up with the crew and immediately headed out to a small community called Bryce Mines, located about fifty kilometers east of Sault Ste. Marie. Jerry had been told that the Bayview Hotel there, a cozy and almost two-hundred-year-old establishment, had numerous reportings of ghostly activity.

The twelve-room mansion was built in the early 1800s and was supposed to have been the summer home of French nobility. There were no guests staying at the gothic hotel at the time the television crew was there. (Not because of the ghosts—the owners were renovating the entire place.) Valkos talked with the current owners, father and son, and found out that there had been numerous incidents: Objects would move across a room of their own accord; a light bulb disappeared out of an overhead socket while people were watching it. Several people had also heard, on many occasions, voices in the distance and a small child or baby crying. This crying had upset the two owners because they had often gone in search of the baby to comfort it but could not find it. Ghostly footsteps were often heard on the second floor when no one was there.

Now, when Valkos investigates a haunted house, one of the first things the first things he looks for is a nonparanormal and logical explanation for whatever is occurring there. If he can't explain it using logical and/or natural occurrences, then he attempts to explain it using the paranormal. He began the investigation by asking the men not only what they had experienced or heard but what their emotions were at the time. Sometimes, if a person is very depressed, he may pick up depressing past energies and ''hear'' sadness from the past. Fear can also contribute to a manifestation. If the person is terrified of seeing a ghost, his own mind may ''create'' a ghostly manifestation to justify his own fears.

The owners of the hotel were a bit startled at first with the spectral comings and goings. They were not afraid of them and after a short period of time got used to them. Valkos felt this was the norm rather than the exception in genuine haunted houses. The living members of the household get quite used to the nonliving members.

After Valkos and MacDermid had interviewed the two men, they went up to the second floor, cameras in hand. Valkos, being a psychic, could pick up vibrations from people and places. He was also a sensitive and could tune in to ghostly manifestations.

While the television crew was shooting on the second floor, Valkos felt something pulling him toward the attic floor. He was a bit unsure as to why, but he felt they were being called up there. The crew followed him into the attic.

Valkos suddenly felt a tremendous sadness and loneliness coming from two separate rooms in the attic. He asked the camera crew and MacDermid to give him a few moments alone. After they had left, Valkos felt, rather than heard, someone crying. There was also a feeling of rejection so intense that it almost broke his heart. He felt that whatever had happened here in the attic, it was the source of the haunting.

The spirit of a young girl appeared to Valkos. The impressions communicated to him by the spirit were that she was a deformed child who was an embarrassment to her family. She told him that her name was Jenny and that she had to live in the attic. She had very little to do with the world outside the house. She was permitted to play outside the house, but only at night—so as not to offend the neighbors.

Valkos was not able to find out exactly what Jenny's deformity was, but he surmised that her face was badly disfigured, almost like a female "elephant man." Jenny lived in the house her entire life and died there, from an illness Valkos couldn't find out (but he suspected it was tuberculosis). Jenny had imprisoned her own spirit in the house and was frightened to leave it.

According to Valkos, this is a common reason why spirits

will haunt a house after they die. Once a spirit realizes it is relatively easy to leave, it will do so. So Valkos told Jenny that there was no reason for her to stay there in the house and she should be free to go whenever she wanted to. He told her to look toward the light and move on. Almost immediately afterward Valkos felt a tremendous sense of relief and saw a small ball of white light leave the house through the ceiling. Unfortunately, he'd sent away the camera crew and never got the light on film. Afterward Valkos had the camera crew come back into the attic. They shot some footage of the room where the ghost child had appeared.

Then the crew also took some footage of the other room at the top of the hotel. It, too, felt as if a great sadness and pain had occurred there. It contained a great deal of negative energy—Valkos's first reaction was to turn around and leave. But he mentally shielded himself and was able to enter the room. He realized that this energy had a totally different feeling to it than the one in Jenny's room. With the cameras rolling, he described his impressions and explained about residue negative energies. He was able to feel that someone, possibly a servant, had committed suicide by hanging and that the death had left negative energy.

These two separate rooms were the cause of the paranormal events in the house. Valkos felt that the crying heard by many persons was a "past-picture" haunting—an event that has happened in the past and repeats itself in the present—and was probably Jenny.

The television crew left and went to several other haunted areas. But they found none were as interesting as the hotel. The television program was aired the following year, 1989, on, of course, Halloween.

While there have been no major paranormal incidents at the hotel since Valkos's visit, one of the owners did report the following: He was in bed and was just waking up when he saw a shadowy form coming toward him. He instantly shouted—and the apparition disappeared. And disembodied voices are still heard in the building. If the ghostly child left the hotel, either she's returned, or another ghost is still in residence. But Valkos has since returned to the hotel and felt happier vibrations. Perhaps Jenny is in a better place, finally playing in the sun.

# The Talking Cat
# of Danville

D anville is a small city in southern Virginia, close to
the North Carolina border. It has grown quite a bit
from its early beginnings, but more than fifty years
ago, when Danville was just a town, something strange happened in an old house there. The exact date is not known,
but it probably happened sometime during the first forty years
of this century.

Off West Main Street in Danville was a ramshackle house
that already enjoyed a reputation for being haunted. Weird
noises were often heard coming from the abandoned house in
the early hours of the morning. And it was said that no lady
could spend the night in the house and survive. The house
was known as the old Ficklen Field place. Its setting was
somewhat isolated: The house was in the midst of a thicket
of briars and trees. It was also located between the town and
a black settlement known as Poor House Hill. The inhabitants
of Poor House Hill refused to walk past the old Ficklen Field
house because of its reputation, although passing it was a
much shorter walk between the settlement and town.

One day a group of boys decided to test the frightening tale that no lady could spend the night in the house and live. They took up a collection; since the blacks at that time were very poor, the most they could raise was one dollar. They offered this dollar to anyone—lady or not—who would spend a night in the old house.

One brave boy named Louis took the challenge. He exclaimed that there were no such things as "haints" and he would prove it. Perhaps he thought that not being a lady increased his chances of winning.

The crowd walked Louis to the outskirts of the house, but would go no nearer. They watched as he gathered up pieces of wood, and later they saw smoke rising from the chimney. When it began to get dark, they hastily left.

The night was cold and wind whistled through the cracks in the walls. Since the house contained a large, open fireplace, the roaring fire warmed the boy. He also had found an old rocking chair near the fireplace, so he dragged it close to the fire. Soon, between the warmth of the fire and the rocking of the chair, he had fallen asleep.

No one knows how long he slept, but as the fire began to die out, Louis awoke.

Pleased with himself for surviving the night, he started mentally spending the prize money. "I knew there were no such things as haints. But I'm sleepy . . . and getting cold."

Then he heard a voice echo, "I'm sleepy and getting cold."

When he looked around, he saw a huge black cat with green eyes—the biggest blackest cat with the greenest eyes he'd ever seen. With a mighty leap, Louis jumped out of the rocking chair and flew out the front door. He ran as fast and as hard as he could for about two miles, then collapsed against a tree.

When he caught his breath, he said out loud, "I'm plumb tired, but I sure did run."

Again the same voice repeated, "I'm plumb tired, but I sure did run."

Looking around, the boy saw the same big black cat with the same green eyes. It just sat there, staring.

The boy muttered, "Looks like I'm gonna run some more—and keep on running."

The cat repeated, "Run some more and keep on running."

The boy took off, and it is said that even today he is still running. When he never came back, the people of Poor House Hill immortalized Louis, the house, and the cat in a song.

The story of Louis and the old Ficklen Field house was gathered by a local reporter in 1940. By then the old house had entirely collapsed from neglect. So it is likely that a new house may have been built in the same location. Perhaps some intrepid investigator can go through the old records at the county clerk's office and find out what is located there now. Perhaps someone can ask the new owners if they've seen any black cats lately. . . .

# The Guardian Angel of Justice

In 1978, two middle-aged sisters, Ethel and Arlene Crestwood (not their real names), moved into a brand-new house in Justice, Illinois. Their house had been built over the location of another house, which had been hauled away when the elderly couple who'd owned it had died in an accident.

The Crestwood sisters were excited about their new home because it was built entirely to their specifications. But no sooner did they move in than odd things started to happen.

A wall telephone in Ethel's bedroom continually would ring—but there was no telephone there! The front door would open by itself. Light switches would go on and off.

One afternoon Ethel was in the house alone, with just the dog for company. After getting dinner ready, Ethel sat down to rest, the dog beside her. She closed her eyes—but something made her open them. She realized the dog was rigidly staring at the hallway and every hair on the dog's body stood up like a pin. In the doorway, just a few feet off the floor, was a misty fog. And a second, smaller mist was rolling down the hallway behind it. Ethel and the dog watched as the two forms went right through a solid wooden door down the hall.

Both sisters began to feel they were not alone in the house. Arlene and Ethel would see the misty forms—usually alerted to their coming by the dog, whose hair would always stand on end.

But the most bizarre occurrence was when Arlene was in the kitchen drinking a cup of coffee. Suddenly a coat—a large man's coat—fell on her.

"Would you please," Arlene complained to her sister, "hang up your coat?"

Only there was no coat. . . .

After a while, the sisters decided to ask their neighbors some questions, thinking their house was somehow haunted by the elderly couple. They found out that the couple had a wall telephone in the kitchen—the location of which corresponded to Ethel's bedroom. Where Arlene felt a coat fall on her probably corresponded to a previous closet.

They couldn't unearth all the details, but they also found out that the elderly couple had died unexpectedly in an accident. Supposedly a gas explosion killed them and severely damaged the building.

As time went by, the sisters began to get used to the ghosts. They were not frightened by the lights going on and off or the appearance of a white fog traveling through walls. In fact, they thought their dog's predictable reaction to it was comical.

But as the years passed, the Crestwood sisters were curious to find out more. Eventually they called in Norman Basile, a ghost hunter in the Chicago area, who brought a psychic with him. However, the sisters made it clear that they were very happy with the ghost—and vice versa.

In walking around the house, both Norman Basile and the psychic felt a presence. Norman called it a "guardian angel," though he didn't know why.

The psychic agreed with Basile. "It's watching over you," she told the sisters, "and it's somebody close to you who passed away."

The sisters explained that their father had died more than fifteen years ago. Their mother died about two years ago; and an older brother had died just months after the mother.

"That's it!" said the psychic. "The smaller cloud is the *younger* brother—I can see him right here. He died in the Navy."

"It's not the people who died in the house?" Basile was surprised. "What's he doing here?"

"He's just wandering around, being comfortable," said the psychic. "He's here because the sisters have been depressed and in ill health for more than a year."

"That's all true," said Arlene. "Ethel's been in the hospital. And we've been disturbed by the loss of our mother and other brother. Ours was a very close family."

Basile asked, "How did the younger brother die?"

"It was during World War II," said Arlene.

"He was on a ship," said the psychic, "but I don't think he died there. I see him standing on a pier and then an explosion. I also see an island in a warm climate."

"He was stationed at Ormond Bay in the South Pacific," said Ethel. "His ship went down during the Battle of Leyte. It was torpedoed—maybe that was the explosion you saw."

"I see his body flying through the air, but I don't see anything after that," said the psychic. "He may not have died; perhaps he was captured."

Ethel fell silent for a moment. "We never knew for certain what happened. But I should tell you about a strange vision I had many years later. I was married and living in California. I kept a picture of my brother in his uniform over my living room fireplace. One night I was dozing on the couch, when something made me open my eyes. The wall opposite me had turned into a scene of the most beautiful waterfall. My younger brother was standing on some rocks next to the waterfall—he was in civilian clothes, not his uniform—and he was staring straight at me and smiling. There was someone standing next to him that I knew was God. That's when I knew he was really dead and in a better place.

"I got off the couch and walked to the stairs, but I turned around to look at my brother's photograph. Over his head was a ball of fire."

We don't know if the sisters are still in their house. But wherever they are, we know a guardian angel is watching over them.

# The Werewolf
# of Lawton

When the U.S. Army recruits soldiers, it usually expects that the enlistees are human. When occult investigator Bradley Sinor researched the following incredible story (all the names have been changed except his), he discovered that no recruiter ever mentioned the possibility of having to share the barracks with a werewolf. . . .

Located in southwestern Oklahoma, Lawton is the third largest city in the state. The town's population of 85,000 is augmented by another 20,000 soldiers stationed at Fort Sill, which is the field artillery training center for the Army and is adjacent to the city. (The base was also a staging and training area for a number of troops involved in Operation Desert Storm.)

Ron Dee had been in the Army for three years when he was assigned to Fort Sill. In February 1971, Dee and his wife, Jackie, had returned to their off-base apartment after having dinner with friends.

As the couple was relaxing for the evening, Jackie realized that she had forgotten to bring in some things from the back porch. Since the weather forecast was for freezing temperatures with a possibility of snow, Jackie thought it would be a good idea to retrieve them.

When she opened the door and stepped out onto the porch, Jackie realized that she was not alone. In the moonlight she saw . . . something. Standing next to the porch was a large humanoid creature whose body was covered with fur, its face a bizarre mixture of wolf and human.

Ron Dee sprinted across the room when he heard his wife's scream. He was at her side in time to see the wolfman leap over the wooden fence that surrounded their backyard and disappear into the darkness, a horrible growling echoing in the cold Oklahoma night.

A later encounter with the creature would not be so benign. Early on the evening of February 27, Matt Dickson heard something out in front of his house. In the late-winter darkness he caught a glimpse of a vaguely humanlike figure kneeling on the front lawn near a nearly empty fish pond.

More curious than scared, Dickson decided to find out who the stranger was. When he stepped out on his front porch for a better look, he felt as if he might have slipped into a 1950s horror film. Attempting to scoop up puddles of water from the bottom of the fish pond was a wolflike man crouched on its hands and knees.

The sight was so shocking that Dickson suffered a heart attack and had to be rushed to Comanche County Memorial Hospital. He was lucky; the heart attack was mild enough for his doctor to release him only two days later, with strict orders for him to go home and rest for several weeks.

In the report taken by a Lawton police officer, Dickson described the creature: "It was tall, with a lot of hair all over its face and body and was dressed in an indescribable manner." Other witnesses that night, and on other evenings, described the wolfman as wearing clothing of some kind.

Some said that he wore both pants and shirt, while others claimed the creature was bare-chested. All of them agreed that the garments were much too small for him. Over the next few evenings the wolfman was seen in a number of locations all over Lawton.

Like most towns located next to a military base, there is an area where businesses cater especially to the off-duty soldiers' needs and entertainment: bars, pizza joints, pawn shops, and Army surplus stores. Known locally as "The Strip," it is a two-mile-long section of 11th Street, just north of Cache Road, that runs directly up to one of the base entrances. At almost the exact center of this corridor is a cemetery that dates back to only a short time after Lawton and Fort Sill were established, at the turn of the century.

Just after midnight, two nights after the wolfman was first seen, a group of young soldiers was heading back to the base. They had been working their way through the various bars: the Gold Dragon, the Spot, and others, doing some very serious celebrating. Completion of the advanced infantry training course is an important event in the careers of new soldiers and all of them had successfully passed the course. So they had a lot of steam to blow off and good reason to celebrate.

While walking along a darkened street near "The Strip," they found themselves face-to-face with the wolfman. The creature leaped out from behind some bushes, screeched at the startled young men, and ran off into the darkness.

One of the soldiers later said that "with more bravery than brains, we chased after it, but lost the thing somewhere near the cemetery."

The phone at the Lawton police department began ringing off the hook over the next several evenings—all reports of sightings of the wolfman.

At first the sightings were coming from a very limited area

of Lawton, but soon the creature was seen all over town. According to a police officer, it would dodge around parked cars, leap into the headlights of oncoming vehicles and then out again at the last minute, and duck in and out of bushes, always growling before running away.

One night, less than twenty minutes after one officer started answering the phone, he received a call from a man who claimed to have had a genuine close encounter with the wolfman.

"The man told me that he saw this 'thing,' as he described it," the officer told Sinor, "when he looked out his apartment kitchen window. At first he suspected the whole thing was somebody's idea of a joke because the creature looked like some kind of monkey or ape."

Only it was no joke. When the man got a look at the creature, he saw a horribly distorted face that looked as if it had been burned in some kind of fire.

As it had when Ron and Jackie Dee first sighted it, the wolfman reacted quickly, leaping from its perch to the ground—nearly twenty feet below—and vanished into the darkness. Only this time it ran away not on two feet, like a man, but on four legs . . . like a wolf.

After so many reports and sightings, a major in the police patrol division sent out an alert for all the policemen to keep an extra-careful watch for the wolfman. That order was to remain in effect until early in the spring of 1971.

In spite of that, or perhaps because of that, the creature was not seen along the streets of Lawton again. Yet even with the passing of years, the file has not been closed. Officially, the Lawton Police Department long ago closed the so-called "Wolfman" case. Unofficially, some officers are willing to admit that the file remains open—inactive, but still open. As for what happened to the wolfman, there have been as many

xplanations offered by local residents as there are people to
xpress them.

Some speculate that the creature may have reverted to its
uman form and just moved on. There are reports of a wolflike
umanoid being spotted in nearby states not too many weeks
fter the Lawton incident. Other people believe that the crea-
ure slipped back across the dimensional rift it had come
hrough, to its own world, wherever or whenever that might
e. Or perhaps its enlistment was up. . . .

Whatever the explanation, even twenty years later there are
till guarded chuckles and uneasy smiles among the older
esidents of the town when the wolfman is mentioned. On
ights when the moon is full, they take an extra look over
heir shoulders, especially if they hear an unnatural howling.

# The Phantom Menagerie

In A.D. 565, a man in dark robes stood upon the shores of the haunted lake and summoned the evil dragon that lived in its murky depths. Soon the loathsome reptilian beast appeared, raising its horned head.

Calling upon the power of prayer and the force of his own will, he battled the dangerous creature, which had already killed one man. He commanded it to depart, and finally the monster slunk away in defeat.

The man was Saint Columba, an Irish prince of the U Neill clan who became a monk. He crossed the Irish Sea to Scotland, where he set about converting the Picts. Banishing the creature in Loch Ness was only one of the miracles he performed, but this particular act so impressed the king of the Picts that he converted to Christianity.

The stuff of legend? Perhaps. . . .

In 1973, a man in black robes once again stood upon the Scottish shores of that haunted lake and summoned the serpent that lived there. The man's name was Reverend Donald Omand and he was conducting an exorcism of the Loch Ness

Monster by visiting several points on the lake where the creature had been sighted.

It seemed like a bizarre idea to some, but attending the exorcism—and believing it necessary—was Ted Holiday. Holiday had done much to further the scientific exploration of Loch Ness. He wrote his first book about it, *The Great Orm of Loch Ness*, in 1968, and thought the creature—now called "Nessie"—was a form of giant aquatic slug.

Having interviewed countless witnesses and spent several weeks on the shore of the loch year after year, Holiday was frustrated. He'd seen increasingly complex searches conducted with sophisticated gear such as underwater cameras, submersibles, and sonar. These searches were supported by various scientific institutions, the military, the British Broadcasting System and the *New York Times*. Yet no concrete evidence of Nessie was uncovered, although the creature was still reported being seen.

Since the 1960s, evidence has mounted that unusually large creatures inhabit Loch Ness. In 1960, Tim Dinsdale, an engineer who would soon become the leading authority on the Loch Ness Monster, photographed it with his movie camera. After that initial sighting, Dinsdale organized a number of expeditions in search of the monster and wrote three books about it.

In 1965, Dr. Roy P. Mackal, a biologist and chemist, began studying Nessie. He felt that the creature was probably a plesiosaur, a prehistoric dinosaurlike reptile with large fins and flippers.

In 1976, the *New York Times* and the Academy of Applied Science mounted yet another expedition. Dennis Meredith, an editor of *Technology Review* who took part in that expedition, thought Nessie was an elasmosaur, another prehistoric creature.

Several photographs support these theories. A famous 1934

photo shows a dinosaur-shaped head and elongated neck rising from the water. A more recent underwater photo shows a large prehistoric-looking animal with flippers.

Joseph W. Zarzynski has been hunting for Champ, the American counterpart to Nessie that lives in Lake Champlain, New York. (For more information, see the story "The Lake Champlain Serpent" in *Dead Zones*.) Zarzynski joined the Loch Ness expeditions and he found an eerie similarity between the two lakes: Both are glacially carved, deep, dark and cold.

While Loch Ness is relatively small, 24 miles long compared to Lake Champlain's 109, there are some areas of Loch Ness that are more than twice as deep—over 900 feet! "One of the problems with Loch Ness," explains Zarzynski, "is that if you get down more than thirty or forty feet, it gets very murky and dark because of the peat in the water."

Perhaps another expedition with technologically advanced cameras may show something. Meanwhile, people along the shores of Loch Ness continue to see things—or do they?

Ted Holiday began to wonder how the Loch Ness Monster could avoid being captured on film when so many people were looking for it. There were many instances where witnesses with cameras didn't use them. Or by the time they managed to snap a picture the creature had vanished. He also found that a number of people reported feelings of dread shortly before or during the sightings. Taking all this into account, Holiday gradually adjusted his theories about Nessie.

Some twenty years after his first book, Holiday wrote *The Goblin Universe*. He thought that Nessie might be more para-normal than physical. It could be an otherworld entity that occasionally manifested itself, or it could be an apparition triggered by the mental state of the witness. Holiday based this theory on other legendary creatures long sought after but never found, such as Bigfoot. He welcomed them into "the safe ark of the Phantom Menagerie where all things are real, provided you define the sort of reality you want."

Holiday wrote about his own investigation of what he called "living apparitions." He went in search of the spirit of the god Pan in Greece. He also went to Ben MacDhui in Scotland, where an apparition is said to haunt this mountain peak. Many experienced mountain climbers reported seeing strange creatures there while a sense of dread overcame them.

Unable to pin down these transitory creatures, and in fact experiencing quite serene feelings at Ben MacDhui, Holiday once again felt he was dealing with the Phantom Menagerie. Yet at one point, Holiday definitely felt there was something inherently evil in Loch Ness.

That was why on June 2, 1973, he accompanied Reverend Donald Omand and a few others to several sites around the lake while the Reverend Mr. Omand blessed them with holy water. While strong winds blew, they rowed out to a spot near Urquhart Castle, where the reverend performed the rites of exorcism.

Holiday was very apprehensive. "If the evil ones could produce manifestations to order, now was the time."

He thought that, based on the party's psychological expectations, the lake should be filled with monsters. But they saw nothing. Internationally known occult researcher John Keel has postulated that people who see strange things—and those of us who want to but don't—are at the mercy of a "cosmic jester."

Shortly after the exorcism, Holiday had a number of peculiar experiences, which he felt were related to alleged UFO sightings in the area by other Loch Ness researchers.

So the hunt goes on. Scotland's haunted lake remains a favorite tourist attraction. There will be more sightings and possibly more photos taken.

As Joseph Zarzynski remarked, "Loch Ness is cold and gloomy at times. . . . It's a very fitting place for a monster. Someone once said that if you look at Loch Ness, if it doesn't have a monster, it *should*."

# The Sweet
# Sixteen Specter

A ntioch Hill Road is a deadly road that twists and winds its way around a crest in the northern Westchester Hills near Antioch, New York, for several miles. In the fall of 1967, a reflecting guard rail and some overhead lights were installed on the north side of the road on the worst stretch, where there's a sheer drop of a hundred feet. Although it's treacherous in damp weather, especially when there's ice or snow or fallen leaves on its surface, no one's been killed there in more than twenty years.

Kids who grew up near Antioch in the mid-sixties remember how the road used to be. Diana Solloway (all the names in this story have been changed) recalls taking its unlit curves at sixty miles per hour on a dare, scared out of her wits, in a car packed with six of her best friends.

The piece of road by the hundred-foot cliff was predictably called Lovers' Leap. Diana's family lived opposite Lovers' Leap in a two-hundred-year-old farmhouse that had a huge oak tree at the edge of the road. It was the only house on

Antioch Hill Road for a two-mile stretch, starting from town and winding past open fields to skirt Falcon Lake. It had been vacant for five years before the Solloways bought and renovated it in 1962.

During the years it was vacant, and because of its location, it had been a hangout for local teenagers. The house was too isolated to interest the local constabulary, so the kids who hung out there were left to their own devices. There were make-out parties galore, and plenty of pranks. The chief thrust of these practical jokes was to terrify the younger kids by convincing them that the house on the Leap was haunted.

But in the five years Diana lived there, no bloodcurdling wails were heard. No evil-faced fiend menaced anyone. By the time Diana was sixteen, she decided the house's mystique was a myth, until the summer of 1967, when Timmy DeLuso died. . . .

Timmy got his driver's license in May, and from the moment he did he was on his motorcycle, racing up and down the road from dawn until way after dusk. He loved that bike, cut school to ride it, and even got a part-time job to keep its gas tank filled.

Timmy had a terrific crush on Diana's best friend, Teena Sherman. But Teena's parents wouldn't allow her to go out with "a motorcycle hoodlum who plays hooky all the time."

Teena was too obedient a daughter to date Timmy on the sly, and if the truth be known, she was afraid of Timmy and his bike. But Timmy was tenacious. He always knew when Teena spent the night at Diana's house and constantly would ride by on his motorcycle.

The Solloways soon knew it was Timmy's bike just by the sound. The low, roaring *vroom, vroom, vroom* he made just before rounding the farmhouse bend was his signature. The elder Solloways spoke to both girls about the disturbances.

and Diana, the bolder of the two, approached Timmy during one of his increasingly rarer appearances at the high school.

"Why don't you leave Teena alone? Her parents won't let her date you, and you're beginning to get on my folks' nerves with the noise. Go ride your damn bike in front of someone else's house."

Timmy just grinned. "It's a free country. If you want quiet, tell Teena to go out with me."

But Teena refused, and Timmy continued to ride past the Solloway house at night. Both girls' parents were on the verge of calling the police when fate intervened.

It was a rainy Friday in June. Both girls had gone out on a double date with "acceptable" boys that night and now Teena was sleeping over. As they were getting ready for bed, they heard that familiar *vroom, vroom, vroom* from about a mile away.

Diana groaned. "It's after midnight. My parents are going to call the cops. They said they would the next time he disturbed us after ten. You've got to talk to him, Teena. Maybe he'll stop if you ask him."

Teena shook her head. "You know I can't go out with him. Besides, I'd never ride on that monster motorcycle."

Then they heard it, a loud squealing of rubber on asphalt, the crunch of metal against metal. Running to the window, they saw the motorcycle lying on the side of the road. Timmy was nowhere to be seen.

He had been thrown from the bike down the side of Lovers' Leap. His neck had been broken, his skull crushed. Teena became hysterical and had to be sedated. She didn't return to school and her parents took her away for the summer.

Diana was badly shaken for days. It was the first time she knew anyone her own age who had died. But she recovered enough to have her own sweet sixteen party as previously planned, the weekend after school let out. Inevitably, at the party the name of Timmy DeLuso was mentioned. Kids wanted to know if Diana had seen anything weird since that night.

Diana explained that all she saw was the wreck right outside her bedroom window, but that was all. Nothing "weird," despite the house's reputation.

"How can you live in a haunted house?" someone asked.

"It isn't haunted," said Diana's mother from the doorway. "And it's past midnight. Good night, boys."

Diana's party had an unusual arrangement. All the boys were to go home by midnight; the girls were to stay over for a slumber party. After the boys left, and Diana's parents had gone to bed, the six girls settled in for the night.

"Let's have a séance," someone suggested.

Another girl asked, "What's that?"

It was explained that a séance was a method to contact the dead. Everyone would sit in a circle, holding hands, and attempt to contact Timmy DeLuso. This was not an appealing pastime for Andrea Dalber, who decided to bake cookies instead.

Andrea went out to the kitchen while the remaining five girls sat in a circle and held hands. The lights had been turned off and only one candle, purloined from the china closet, was lit.

Everyone closed their eyes. One girl intoned, "We call of the spirit of the dear, departed Timothy DeLuso. Come to us, Timothy. Speak to us from the other side."

For several minutes there was silence. Nothing happened. Then Diana felt a sensation of absolute cold coming from the center of the circle. She opened her eyes and saw a translucent white form hovering there.

Without thinking, she reached toward it, then realized she had broken the circle. She tried to withdraw her hand, but couldn't. It was frozen in place as though something were holding her wrist. "Oh, my God," Diana screamed. "My hand is stuck, I can't move it."

All the girls started screaming hysterically. The figure drifted away, backing off until it disappeared through the hall doorway. As it crossed the boundary of the circle, Diana felt her hand get warm again. She could move it. She jumped to her feet, running after the figure.

"Please come back," she cried. "We aren't really frightened." But it was gone. The other girls were all around her, crying and babbling.

At the sound of so much noise, Andrea returned. She hadn't seen anything in the hallway and had no idea what was going on. Diana had the presence of mind to calm everyone down and then send them into the kitchen, one by one, to tell their versions of the event to Andrea. Then they would compare notes.

In ten minutes they had finished. A pale and shaky Andrea was in the living room telling them, "You're either putting this on to scare me, or you all saw the same thing: a white figure that floated out of the circle into the hall. Tell me you're joking."

"I think I'm going to be sick." Diana raised her hand to cover her mouth.

One of the girls gasped and pointed to Diana. Diana looked over her shoulder. "Did it come back?"

"No, look at your hand."

Around Diana's wrist was a bright red mark, like a bruise. The next day it was black and blue. It took several weeks to fade away, and until it did, Diana constantly felt the presence of someone just behind her. But when she looked, no one was ever there.

Diana later told this story to her friend Roberta Klein-Mendelson. Diana still believed her house wasn't haunted and Roberta wasn't sure she believed the ghost story, anyway. But as the two friends grew up, their situations reversed in the most unusual way: A ghost showed up in Roberta's home (see "The House on Clover Street" in *Dead Zones*) and Diana eventually lived in a genuine haunted house that Roberta exorcised (see "Spectral Restorations" this volume).

# Stay Out
# of Room 310

Columbia, Missouri, is a bustling college town that on the surface, at least, seems about as ghost-free as anyplace on earth. But it has at least one ghost that has generated a lot of interest in the community. It's been the subject of several newspaper articles and usually earns a couple of minutes of television coverage each year, often on Halloween. Yet few in town, especially the reporters who cover the story, take it very seriously.

The men of the Sigma Phi Epsilon fraternity are less amused. They have to live with the ghost, and lately she's been pretty busy. Indeed, virtually every classic symptom of spirit infestation is said to be present in the house: cold spots, discarnate voices, poltergeist activity, even the occasional apparition of something described as a "girl made out of ivory."

The haunting goes back to the 1940s, a time when the house was the temporary property of a Jewish sorority. As the legend goes, a young girl hanged herself after learning that her parents had died in a German concentration camp.

She tied a rope around a radiator and threw herself from the window of her third-floor room.

Most of the psychic activity centers on room 310, which was where the tragedy allegedly took place. Current residents refer to it as the "ghost room," though physically there is absolutely nothing spooky about it. There's modern carpeting on the floor, fresh paint on the walls. A single large window provides more than adequate sunlight. Two bunk beds are suspended on stilts to make room for desks, chairs, and the clutter that inevitably accumulates in such a place.

In short, 310 is exactly the kind of room you'd expect to find in a large, noisy fraternity house. It's small, cramped, and utterly mundane. Yet anyone who stays for any length of time always has a story or two to tell regarding their own experiences.

Greg Raeman lived in the room in 1988. Up to that point, his life had not been complicated by the supernatural and he wasn't about to believe in something as intangible as a ghost. Yet today Raeman sings a different tune. Strange things happened to him in room 310, events that even now he isn't particularly anxious to talk about.

One of the more interesting, if somewhat embarrassing, incidents took place as he was getting ready for a party one night.

"I went to take a shower and came back to the room wearing a towel," he said. "One of my roommates, Joe Raithel, had been in the room but left when I came back. As I started changing, I heard a girl giggling. I thought Joe had let my girlfriend in and not told me about it. I looked around, thinking she was hiding in the closet or something as a joke. She wasn't, so I climbed up and checked out the top of the bunk beds. Again, nothing.

"I called for Joe, but he didn't hear me, though he was right outside the door. I went out and asked him if he'd hidden someone in the room or if anyone had been in the room and left. He said no, so we both searched the room but found nothing. It was weird. I'd have sworn on my life there'd been a girl in the room.''

1988 was a big year for the "girl made out of ivory." Scott Calvi and Joe Raithel, who occupied the room after Raeman vacated it, reported a number of disquieting incidents. One of these involved a wicker chair that would creak during the night as though someone were sitting down in it and getting up again. Late one evening, when Calvi was away, Raithel woke up suddenly. He'd heard more than just a chair creaking; he heard footsteps and odd rustling noises.

"My bed was right next to the chair," he said with an edge of fear in his voice. "And I knew there couldn't be anybody in the room. I looked down and there wasn't anybody there. It was pretty scary."

Calvi and Raithel also complained of excessive heat in the room. Even in the dead of winter, with the window open and the ceiling fan going full blast, it would remain hot as a sauna. Stranger still, the old steam radiator had never worked properly and couldn't possibly generate that much heat.

The building has been renovated several times and the window the girl threw herself from has since been closed up. The radiator sits next to the place where the window used to be. Legend has it that rapping three times on the radiator will summon the ghost.

For right now, however, no one seems anxious to put it to the test.

There are many other tales connected with room 310, many of which reveal the spirit's mischievous side. She seems inordinately fond of annoying people.

Greg Bryson, a recent occupant of the room, was often the target of her pranks. "One night we were sleeping and my roommate decided to get up and go outside. When he came back, the door was locked. He didn't lock it when he left and I was still asleep. He had to wake me up to get back inside. We have no idea how the door got locked. It was like someone was playing a game.''

Other recent incidents reveal another facet of the ghost's personality. Evidently she's got a serious side. And she doesn't care to be mocked.

One resident loudly proclaimed that he didn't believe in the "damn ghost." He was immediately rebuked, as a mirror that had been firmly anchored to the wall went crashing to the floor.

Scott Calvi tells a similar story. Right after he moved in, he asked his roommate Joe Raithel if he believed in the spirit. "I don't believe in that bitch," Raithel replied insolently. Almost at once, a wall hanging bearing the fraternity's insignia of a skull and crossbones mysteriously detached itself and fluttered to the floor.

Still another resident foolishly challenged the spirit as he and a friend were working with a computer. "If the ghost wants to come and get me, let it try." At that moment the screen went blank. Nothing was wrong with the computer; the plug had not been pulled from the wall socket. The machine had simply switched itself off.

The "girl made out of ivory" does not restrict her activities to room 310. She sometimes stops to admire herself in front of a full-length mirror at the end of the third-floor hallway. Cold spots have often been reported in that vicinity and many have had the misfortune to see her, including Scott Calvi.

One night, as he was coming out of the bathroom, he saw a white mist at the end of the hallway. The mist was directly in front of the hallway mirror. Calvi felt no compulsion to study the apparition. Instead he practically flew down the stairway in his haste to get away from it.

A more frightening story concerns a hapless fellow who

once remained in the house after everyone else had gone to a party. After he had taken a shower that night, the young man went back out into the hallway and found all the lights flickering. "Hey, guys, quit messing around," he said, assuming someone had stayed behind to play a trick on him.

As the words left his mouth, the ghost materialized in front of the mirror and lunged at him. The man ducked, but the apparition touched his neck as it passed overhead and left something on his skin that resembled a burn mark. Quite shaken, the fellow bolted from the house and stood quivering on the front lawn until someone showed up many hours later to escort him back inside.

Flickering lights often herald a ghostly materialization. During spring break, holidays, and the summer months, the ghost will sometimes switch on the lights, perhaps simply to draw attention to herself. This usually creates quite a stir, since everyone knows the house is generally unoccupied at those times.

In the summer of 1989, the rooms were leased to summer students. All of them decided to go bar-hopping together one night and carefully turned off all the lights and locked the doors and windows. They had all left together and had all come home together. Yet when they got back, all the third-floor lights were burning.

If the suicide is a myth, it's a remarkably consistent one, for nothing unusual occurred in the house before World War II. Completed in 1926, the imposing red brick structure was the first to be built for a fraternity on the university campus. It was used as a postal depot from 1941 to 1944, then sold to Sigma Phi, the Jewish sorority. For reasons unknown, the house was sold back to Sigma Phi Epsilon just a few years later.

Hollywood could not have created a more suitable environment for things to go bump in the night. The enormous old house stands tall and formidable on the corner of Kentucky and Providence avenues. It sports long Gothic windows and a sprawling front porch. The main entrance is set back several feet from the roof of the structure and is crowned by a stone arch. The roof is peaked, gabled, and crumbling in sections. With a grim-faced gargoyle or two to stand watch over the downspouts, Sigma Phi would be nearly perfect, at least as haunted houses go.

Inside, there's a huge reception area with tall, wood-beamed ceilings and carpeted marble floors. A massive stone fireplace sets off the room. The mantel is done in scrollwork with the head of a tiger carved in the middle. The furniture gathered around the fireplace is plush and traditional, the ideal place to sit down with friends on a stormy night and share ghost stories.

The upstairs has been completely apportioned into living and sleeping quarters. The corridors are well lit and inviting, the rooms small and cozy. Downstairs there's a gloomy old basement complete with unpleasant bare-bulb lighting and musty odors. The basement is immense. It serves as storage and houses the laundry facilities. Nothing unusual is said to have occurred here, though it seems the perfect setting for weird happenings.

The sound effects in Sigma Phi are great. The floors groan, the doors creak, the furnaces rattle and wheeze. The steps in the cavernous, wood-paneled stairwell protest as you mount them. Old timbers moan and complain as the house settles on its foundation.

Many toss off the ghost stories as manifestations of these very natural phenomenon. Yet Sigma Phi alumni swear by the accounts and speak of supernatural incidents occurring in the house as early as 1948. Some of these tales are much more interesting than the recent ones, but there are still remarkable similarities between them.

The earlier tales include a pair of bobbing red lights that suddenly materialized on the third floor, phantom footsteps racing down the hallways and up the stairs, an appearance of the ghost in the hallway mirror, pipes banging where there were no pipes, and several dramatic events that supposedly took place in the then unchristened "ghost room."

In room 310, the windows are said to have broken, even to have blown out, for no apparent reason. Residents have been awakened in the middle of the night when someone called their name or shook their shoulder, only to find that there was no one else in the room. The "girl made out of ivory" sometimes materialized by the door and approached people as they were lying in their beds.

A phantom whirlwind once created so much pressure that three persons were required to open the door. Breathing and moaning noises, a staple of any good ghost story, were also reported, along with objects that suddenly became airborne and moved about under their own power. One person was even said to have gone into a trance in the room as he was talking to friends. The trance lasted until midnight, the very hour of the girl's alleged suicide.

Sigma Phi Epsilon is a periodic haunting. Before the 1980s, no unusual activity had been reported in the house for almost ten years. There could be a perfectly practical reason for this. The seventies were not good years for fraternities and sororities. Only recently have they come back into vogue.

Based on her behavior, it's pretty clear that the ghost of Sigma Phi Epsilon likes to perform in front of an audience.

And the bigger the audience, the better she likes it.

# The Kern City Poltergeist

For Dr. Stafford Betty, a psychic investigator and college professor, it all began in January 1982. Dr. Betty is a serious student of the paranormal and, as a result of a phone call, spent a year investigating a very unusual house in Bakersfield, California. (All the names have been changed with the exception of Dr. Betty's.)

On January 27 a woman phoned Dr. Betty, explaining that a friend of hers was "in trouble." The friend, Ethel Kramer, was a widow living in a retirement community called Kern City. If Ethel couldn't find out what was wrong with her house—which she'd bought only months earlier—she was going to sell it!

The house was a white, single-story, three-bedroom home left vacant for five years since the death of the previous owner, Mary Carter. Mary's daughter left the house untouched, so that when Ethel moved in, in November 1981, she found the house nearly as Mary had left it in 1976. Ethel found Carter family pictures hung on the walls, furniture exactly in place,

Mary's clothing in the closets, even Mary's underwear in dresser drawers.

Ethel moved in on November 30, an all-day affair. Mary's daughter and son-in-law came to check on things, offering Ethel a vanity bench that once belonged to Mary. Ethel took the bench and put it in front of a built-in dressing table in the master bedroom. The movers had just left, around ten P.M., when Ethel heard peculiar noises from the kitchen. She decided it was the furnace and went to bed.

The next morning, Ethel found some bedroom doors, which she had carefully closed the night before, standing open. She thought there might be a draft blowing them open and called a repairman to weatherstrip the house.

Ethel also noticed that the vanity bench was pulled out; for the next several days, the vanity bench, carefully pushed under the dressing table, was always out and "in the way" a little later. By the fourth day, Ethel had had enough and stored the bench in the garage. Within a week of moving in, Ethel had transformed the house: new furniture, new carpeting, and, most significantly, two changes in the kitchen. Where a dinette set had been, Ethel installed a long counter with a cabinet of sliding drawers and hinged doors underneath. She also put in a new sink, raised the counter on either side of the sink, and replaced the counter tile with Formica.

On her second night in the house, at around nine-thirty, Ethel heard strange noises again, coming from the kitchen. Again she dismissed them and went to bed. That night she slept on a couch in the living room because of back problems. She carefully closed all the doors in the house.

The next morning, all five doors inside the house were open. Furthermore, all of the doors and drawers in the newly installed kitchen cabinet were open. Ethel called in the repairman and the carpenter, but they found nothing wrong.

For the next two months, each morning Ethel would get up and find all the hallway doors, the sliding kitchen doors, and the cabinet drawers open. Occasionally she experimented by opening the doors and drawers herself before going to bed. The next morning, she'd find them all closed!

Her little dog Missie also exhibited unusual behavior. Missie would be sound asleep, then would perk up her ears, run down the hall, and scratch on a door, as though someone were calling her. Other times, she'd rush across the room and cock her head back and forth, as if responding to a call. She had never done this before. Also, Ethel knew that Missie would bark only at other animals, never at people. During this odd behavior, Missie never barked at all.

In just a few weeks after moving in, the sewer system fell apart, the garage door broke, and the lights would turn themselves on and off. Whenever the electrician replaced one switch, another would act up. Ethel, convinced she'd bought a lemon of a house, called Mary's son-in-law to complain. He was surprised to hear of the calamities and said they'd never had any problems with the house.

"It's almost as though the house is complaining about you being there," he remarked.

Ethel continued to decorate her new house. She hung an old framed print on a wall. The picture was of three Civil War ladies, each framed in an oval. The next morning, the picture was no longer hanging on the nail but was placed neatly on the floor, leaning against the wall. Ethel attempted to hang the picture in several places. Each morning, the picture would be found leaning against the wall. Finally Ethel wandered around the house, looking for just the right place to hang it—almost as if something were directing her. She chose an unlikely spot near a wall switch, hung the picture, and was relieved to find it still in place the next morning. Over the next month or so, if she removed the picture, the disturbances increased. Ethel angrily banished the picture to the garage.

By now Ethel was suspicious that she was sharing her house with a discontented and sometimes boisterous spirit who occasionally sounded as though it were throwing a tantrum in the kitchen. Ethel became certain of it on January 25, 1982—the most terrifying night of her life. That night, after going to bed, she was awakened by a ruckus in the kitchen. Since this had happened before, she went back to sleep. A little while later, Ethel awoke to go to the bathroom. While there, something unseen opened the bathroom window. Ethel closed it.

Confused, Ethel went into her bedroom and sat on the bed, wondering what was going on. Suddenly her bedroom window slammed shut, and at the same time the bathroom window slammed open. Almost immediately, the activity shifted to two closets near the bed. At the exact time that the folding doors of one closet opened, those of the other closed. Missie stood on the bed yapping, her head swiveling from closet to closet.

*I've got to get out of here!* Ethel thought.

Heart racing, she grabbed Missie and ran down the hall. But then she felt an impact—there was something ominous and ugly there.

Terrified, Ethel yelled "Get out of my way!" and charged through. (Later she told Dr. Betty that she felt *three* ghosts in the hallway as she passed through.) Throwing a coat over her nightgown, she jumped into her car and drove away.

Dr. Stafford Betty agreed to investigate the house in Kern City. He brought along two women colleagues, both psychics. The house was examined for natural explanations, but none were found.

While he and the two women were examining the house, suddenly Ethel screamed. They rushed in to find that Ethel had seen a dining chair move of its own accord. It had been placed away from the table at a forty-five-degree angle. But it slowly turned and pulled itself up against the table as if some invisible hand were "straightening up." Dr. Betty was skeptical, but upon closer investigation he noticed four clear indentations on the thick carpet where the rollers of the chair apparently sat moments before.

The rest of the afternoon—an hour and a half—went more smoothly. Both psychics said the manifestations were obviously coming from the former owner, Mary Carter. They could "see" three spirits in the house: an older couple and a sad, lost young woman. It was theorized that the older couple might be Mary Carter reunited with her late husband; who the girl was, no one knew.

The two psychics spoke to the spirits, trying to explain that the spirits had passed on but were still attached to a place here on earth. They needed to move on, to the next plane of existence.

Dr. Betty also recommended that Ethel retrieve the tri-oval picture of the Civil-War ladies and hang it in the spot where it "belonged."

A strange thing happened that night—nothing. No doors and drawers opened, the ghosts made no noises. Not quite trusting this turn of events, a fully clothed Ethel slept on the living room couch, with the keys in the car and the garage door open—just in case she needed to flee for her life. Fortunately, the poltergeists did not return.

Many years have passed since this story happened. It is possible that Ethel no longer lives in the modest house in Kern City and the tri-oval picture no longer hangs in its proper spot. In that case, the poltergeists might decide to come back. . . .

# Elementals,
# My Dear Watson

In 1962, when he was ten years old, Bruce Hallenbeck was playing in the woods behind his grandparents' home in Kinderhook, New York. With him was his cousin Sherry. The time was around sundown when Bruce heard a high-pitched whistling sound coming from a nearby pine tree.

Bruce turned to look in the direction of the strange sound and was shocked to see a bluish white blob peering at him from behind the tree. Sherry saw it, too. When Bruce turned to her, she was already halfway down the hill, running in fright toward their grandparents' house. It didn't take long for Bruce to follow.

Bruce passed off the incident as a figment of his imagination. But two years later his friend Jerry Miller came running out of those same woods one day, looking as pale as a ghost himself.

Jerry said that he'd been walking near the spring down in the forest off McCagg Road when he heard something walking behind him. Jerry turned to see a white "blob," as big as a man, moving slowly down the hill in his direction. He was so terrified by the sight of this unearthly entity that he jumped clear over a six-foot-wide pond.

Bruce was excited; Jerry had just described what Bruce had seen two years earlier, but Bruce had never told Jerry about the incident. Both boys decided to go back to the woods together, brandishing "weapons": a pitchfork and a shovel.

They were headed toward the spring when Jerry stopped in his tracks and, yelling excitedly, pointed straight ahead to a bunch of trees. Floating between the trees was a white blob with a bluish haze around it. Bruce and Jerry dropped their weapons and ran.

As the years went by, Bruce and Jerry continued to investigate the woods, but they didn't see the blob again. They did find some old cow bones when they were digging around, but nothing else. However, there were certain areas in the woods—especially near the spring, ponds, and stream—where they felt very apprehensive.

The blob was not reported again until 1978, when two young boys were camping in the woods. Barry Scott and Russell Lee had built a lean-to and were sitting inside it on a fine, clear day. They heard something tramping down the hill. When they looked out of the lean-to to see what it was, they saw something that floated more than it walked.

What's interesting is that each boy saw something different. Barry, who was Protestant, saw only a "bell-shaped, white being." Russell, who was Catholic, saw something he described as "like the Virgin Mary."

Whatever it was, the entity vanished among the trees, leaving the two boys in a state of bewildered excitement.

In 1984, about a week before Halloween, Bruce Hallenbeck's father, a well-to-do and down-to-earth businessman, saw a "white, round, or disclike shape" swoop down from the field behind his house on Novak Road. It zoomed over the road, zipped through the cornfield, and vanished behind the hill. Mr. Hallenbeck was, needless to say, mystified.

All these sightings took place in exactly the same area as sightings of the "Kinderhook Creature," actually sort of a Bigfoot. The creature has been sighted on more than one occasion. UFOs have also been seen nearby and even some "human" ghosts have been reported as well. Kinderhook seems to be the focal point of several kinds of unusual activity.

But what of the "blobs"? It is thought that these are "elementals," a primal being connected with one of the four elements: earth, air, fire, and water. The area in which these are seen is a pleasant tract of land off a well-traveled country road. The Hallenbecks' property encompasses eight acres of wood, field, and pond, with a freshwater spring deep in the woods. Scientist and psychic investigator Sir William Brookes defined elementals in these words: "A separate order of beings, living on this earth, but invisible and immaterial to us. Able, however, to occasionally manifest their presence. Known in almost all countries and ages as demons (not necessarily bad), gnomes, fairies, kobolds, elves, goblins, Puck, etc."

An English dowser named Tom Lethbridge was convinced that there are various types of "earth fields" connected with elementals. Water fields he called "naiad fields," open space and mountains were "oread fields," and woodlands were "dryad fields." Each was named after a different kind of elemental spirit. Lethbridge believed that they were properties of the field—not real spirits, but rather psychic recordings that can only be picked up by sensitive people.

Interestingly, the Kinderhook elemental is associated not only with water but with dowsing. Bruce Hallenbeck's grandfather George was a dowser, and just before Jerry Miller's

encounter, George had found a spring in the forest by dowsing. In fact, the pond that Jerry jumped over was originally
underground water discovered by George Hallenbeck and
brought to the surface after he had dowsed for it.

Bruce Hallenbeck has become a very active investigator of
the occult and paranormal. He has assisted cryptozoologists
in their search for the Lake Champlain creatures. And he has
spent fifteen years personally investigating numerous occult
cases primarily located in upstate New York. Recently he
wrote, directed, and coproduced a feature film, *Vampyre*.

So it came as no surprise that Bruce decided to look for
the Kinderhook elemental once more. On Halloween 1987,
Bruce and some friends decided to try to find out just what
was in the woods. They built a lean-to for protection. With
the help of a Ouija board, the participation of eyewitness
Russell Lee, and a medium from Albany, they succeeded in
contacting . . . something.

Also present was psychic John Brent, who has successfully
experimented with astral projection. However, he'd had a
nasty experience with a Ouija board when he and another
medium conjured up something unpleasant. As a result, Brent
was reluctant to go through with Bruce's experiment; but, as
a friend, he did it.

Brent asked the Ouija board, "Are there any spirits in this
forest?"

The answer was a resounding yes.

The next question was, "Are they spirits of the dead?"

The answer was an equally definite no.

Hallenbeck asked, "Are these spirits elementals?"

The planchette moved slowly toward yes.

"How many are there?"

Six, was the reply.

"Are they good or evil?"

According to the Ouija, they were neither. They were just part of nature—or "supernature."

Hallenbeck and his friends left the lean-to at three in the morning, exhausted but somewhat elated. The group felt they had really contacted something and that they had really been given information.

Bruce Hallenbeck continues to gather information about the Kinderhook area. He feels there's no doubt that some areas seem more haunted than others. Ancient Indian pottery was discovered near the spring in the woods off McCagg Road in the 1940s. He wonders if this area could have been special to Native Americans.

As for why Russell Lee and Barry Scott saw different things, Bruce offers this explanation: Most people perceive things with preconceived notions. And elementals tend to give their "audience" what they expect to see anyway.

But no matter what you see when you're walking in the woods off McCagg Road, please be sure to tell Bruce.

# The Apparition
## at Lourdes

The town of Lourdes in southwest France is located at the foothills of the Pyrenees Mountains. It did not spring to prominence until the mid-1800s, when an apparition repeatedly appeared to a young girl there.

Bernadette Soubirous was born in 1844 to a middle-class Catholic family who eventually squandered their inheritance by the time Bernadette was eleven. The next year, 1856, Bernadette barely survived a cholera epidemic and was left with chronic asthma. For the next several years, because money was scarce, she worked at odd jobs and lived with relatives or foster families. Bernadette was known to be a pleasant girl, not particularly religious, and somewhat backward. So the events of 1858 involving Bernadette were rather startling. . . .

On Thursday, February 11, thirteen-year-old Bernadette, her sister Toinette, and a friend Jeanne, were wandering through the woods and meadows. The other two girls gaily crossed a stream, but Bernadette was left behind, afraid to go into the water because of her asthma.

The stream was not far from a grotto at the foot of the cliff of Massabielle. Bernadette walked near the grotto, planning to sit down and take off her shoes and stockings and then attempt to cross the stream. A noise made her look up. She saw a young girl dressed in a white dress and veil, a blue sash, and a yellow rose on each foot. The vision made the sign of the cross and disappeared.

A shaken Bernadette finished removing her shoes and stockings and fearlessly crossed the stream. Her sister pried the story out of her, and several days later they and a group of friends went back to the grotto. Bernadette was carrying holy water to throw at the apparition in an attempt to exorcise it. When it appeared, she was the only one who could see it. She threw the holy water, but it had no effect. Instead, Bernadette went into an ecstatic trance and had to be carried back home.

The townspeople speculated that the "girl in white" was a ghost, and so at the next encounter Bernadette was accompanied by two women carrying a portable desk. The apparition was asked to write its name.

"That isn't necessary," it replied, and then added, "I don't promise to make you happy in this world, but in the next."

The locals decided these were not the words of a ghost. So on the next visit to the grotto, Bernadette was accompanied by a group of approximately ten women, all of whom witnessed her trance—but not the apparition—and all of whom continued to spread tales about the grotto's strange events. Each time Bernadette went back to the grotto, the crowd with her increased from tens to hundreds to thousands. The police, the local politicians, and of course the Church became involved as the sightings of the apparition continued.

The crowds watched as Bernadette carried on a conversation with or prayed rapturously to an invisible being. On February 25, during the apparition's ninth appearance, Bernadette's behavior suddenly changed. She scampered from her usual spot and climbed down the slope. The apparition had instructed her, "Go and drink at the spring and wash in it."

Since there was no spring, Bernadette thought the lady meant the stream. But, walking back and forth from the cave to the stream, as though following directions, Bernadette eventually returned to the grotto, where she dug into the earth with her hands. The hole filled with muddy water, which she drank and used to wash her face.

The little muddy pool soon turned into a clear spring. People started drinking from the spring or taking bottles of water home with them. A woman from a nearby town washed her injured hand in the waters and recovered the use of her paralyzed fingers. This was the beginning of the controversy about the many alleged miracle cures to come.

All of the pilgrims to the grotto, and later to the basilica built there, began claiming miraculous cures—thousands of cures! But were these really miracles?

Back then, medical knowledge was uncertain. Maladies such as psychosomatic illness, hysteria, and autosuggestion were barely understood. There was no systematic control of medical records. No tests were done under laboratory conditions.

As a result, eminent men of the day (such as Émile Zola) argued intensely about Lourdes. One young doctor, Alexis Carrel, was quite taken with the idea of the miraculous waters and decided to see for himself what the commotion was all about. He felt that if such extraordinary cures were taking place, it was a great opportunity for scientific investigation. So in July 1903 Carrel boarded a train for Lourdes.

He talked to everyone on the train, young and old, sick and well—including an old classmate he ran into—and took notes about his trip. When it was learned that he was a doctor,

he was asked to help take care of the more seriously ill
pilgrims on the train.

There was one deathly ill young girl named Marie Bailly
to whom Carrel gave a morphine injection to ease her pain.
Carrel examined Marie and also took a history of her and her
family from the nun accompanying her. Marie was emaciated
and had a distended stomach, an ashen pallor, and trouble
breathing. She had been quite ill for about eight months, and
for a short while during the train ride, she lapsed into a coma.

The young doctor concluded that Marie Bailly suffered
from tubercular peritonitis and he agreed with her previous
doctors' assessments that Marie's case was hopeless.

Carrel was so sure Marie's condition was organic and not
psychological that he told his friend, "If this girl is cured,
I'll become a monk!"

The train took several days to reach Lourdes and Marie
was worried that she wouldn't survive the trip. She did survive, but she had to be carried from the train on a stretcher.

At Lourdes, Dr. Carrel busied himself with research, talking to his old classmate and doctors at the local hospital. He
watched as volunteers carried sick pilgrims to the grotto.
Carrel knew that Marie Bailly desperately wanted to bathe in
the grotto's waters, but she needed to be carried there. There
was some worry that Marie might not even survive being
brought there on a stretcher. Carrel and other doctors examined her and she appeared to be dying, so Carrel did what he
could for her. Then he sat by the grotto watching the pilgrims,
hoping to see one of the much-talked-about miraculous cures.

By the time Marie Bailly's stretcher was brought to the
water, she was unconscious. Instead of bathing her in the
water, one of the volunteers simply poured a cup or two of
water over the girl's swollen abdomen.

Carrel was watching the other people when he happened

to glance at Marie's stretcher. Startled, he swore he noticed a change in her condition. The harsh shadows of her emaciated face had disappeared and the pallor of her skin was less ashen. He noted the time was twenty to three in the afternoon.

Thinking it might be a hallucination, he asked another doctor to examine Marie. This doctor took her pulse and announced it was less rapid, but he could see no other change. So Carrel looked away and began to watch one of the nuns pray. When he looked back at Marie, Carrel suddenly paled. The blanket covering Marie's distended abdomen was gradually sinking! When the bells of the basilica struck three o'clock, the blanket was flat.

When Carrel examined Marie, there was no longer any sign of her distended stomach. Her pulse had become regular, and she was awake and talking. Carrel was astounded: Marie was cured! Two other doctors present also examined Marie and agreed with him. Witnessing a miracle was a milestone in Carrel's career and he won a Nobel prize just ten years after his trip to Lourdes.

The vision seen by Bernadette had asked that a chapel be built there. The Basilica of the Immaculate Conception was completed in 1871. Its magnificent spires rise dramatically by the Gave de Pau River, and it also descends into a huge subterranean hall. The Grotto has been made more accessible and water from the spring is piped into baths.

The grotto water has been analyzed and it is different from the rest of the natural water in the area. The other water contains a lot of iron; the grotto water does not. But chemical analysis of the grotto water shows that it is nothing more than good-quality drinking water: There is nothing unusual about it to scientifically explain the miracles.

Though in recent years the furor about Lourdes has died down to a whisper, it is said that the miraculous cures continue. There is still controversy over just how many real cures have occurred, but the Catholic church has recognized over thirty cures as being authentic. Lourdes is open to the public year-round. It can be reached by train, car, and bus from the city of Tarbes northeast of the grotto.

# The Parkway Phantom

New Jersey's Garden State Parkway is a 173-mile-long superhighway linking New York state in the north with Delaware's Cape May-Lewes ferry in the south. Built in a day short of three years and opened in July 1955, the parkway passes through ten counties and fifty municipalities as diverse as geography and demography could possibly make them.

The northern end threads through the foothills of the Ramapo Mountains down through industrial New Jersey and eventually slides through the lonely scrub and lost villages of the Pine Barrens. While the northern areas of the parkway harbor little to write about, the southern end seems alive with unusual stories of "encounters." One of the most active centers of strange and inexplicable happenings surrounds the busy and densely congested Route 37 exit at Toms River. It is here that there have been numerous reports of terrifying close calls with what can only be called the Parkway Phantom.

The phantom shows up sporadically, and often witnesses are confused about what they've seen. The reason for the confusion is the fleeting nature of the apparition, or perhaps we should say the fleeting circumstance of the viewers driving it. The phantom is seen only at night, and only on the north-bound side of the Garden State Parkway in an eight-mile stretch straddling Exit 82. The phantom has been reported in the vicinity of the Toms River Barracks of the New Jersey State Police, who have no "official" records of such incidents.

There are two types of sightings. The first type dates back to the days following the opening of the parkway in the fall of 1955.

George Selkirk had traveled to the precasino Atlantic City for a short vacation with his wife Mary and his sons Joshua, age eight, and Martin, age ten (the family's names have been changed for this story). Though they had wanted to start their return trip early, the Selkirks were sidetracked by the lure of seafood and had stayed for dinner in Atlantic City. When they got on the parkway and started north from Exit 40 at Absecon, it was dark and a fog was working its way in from the sedge-filled swamps that bordered the Atlantic Ocean.

They were driving at between forty and forty-five miles an hour through ground fog north of Toms River when George reported seeing the apparition. It happened very suddenly, and since Mary and the boys were asleep there was no corroboration for George's experience. But when Prof. Gene Snyder spoke to him during his investigation of the phantom some thirty-five years after the event, George remembered it clearly . . . and chillingly.

The fog had thinned and George had accelerated slightly, when he thought he saw a figure in the weeds to the right side of the road. He slowed so that he might have time to react if the figure tried to cross the road in front of him. He flipped on his high beams and was greeted with a wall of reflected fog. He snapped back to low beams and slowed further still.

The man was very tall and lean. George's best estimate is that he was six-foot-four or -five. The man did not move; he simply faced the oncoming car and stared as if unsure what to do. He had on a long topcoat that was belted at the waist and a hat that George thinks was a snap-down cap. When George slowed and came abreast of the man, he could see the man raise his right arm and wave as if to flag the car down. George thought there might be a chance the man had been in an accident and the car wreck could not be seen in the fog. Not sure where the accident might be, and on the chance that he might be able to help, George brought the car to a stop. At this Mary awakened, though the boys remained asleep in the back seat.

George reported that he could not have been more than a hundred yards past the figure when he came to a stop on the service lane and started to back up. But the man was gone. There was no disabled car . . . no man . . . nothing but the fog.

Mary asked why they had stopped, and George explained the incident to her. They drove on, and they would not have thought of the incident again if it were not for what happened the following spring.

George was invited to a business convention in Atlantic City and again found himself returning north on the parkway on a Sunday night. On this trip the weather was clear and there was a full moon to light the grassy strips that bordered the area of Toms River north of Exit 82 and south of the state police barracks.

George saw him again.

The man was on the same side of the road, dressed in the same coat and hat, and was raising a hand in the air as if to wave down a car. After a split second of shock, George screeched to a halt and threw the car into reverse.

Again, the man was gone.

In the three and a half decades that he has been driving on the parkway, George has not been able to explain his experiences.

In the second type of sightings, the same man wears ragged clothes—not period costume but contemporary. He stands in much the same place on the side of the road and waves, this time with both hands above his head. The arms wave synchronously, both bending from the elbow in opposite directions at once, like a strange football cheer.

As he waves with the strange arm movements, he walks onto the road surface. Observers have swerved to avoid hitting him, and though there are no official ghost-connected accidents, a great deal of rubber has been left there at night.

Sylvia Zyphrin (not her real name) almost rolled over her then-new 1966 Mustang when she headed north from her mother's home in Beach Haven. It was a clear March evening, just past eleven, and Sylvia was going home to her apartment in Brick Township.

Sylvia saw a man on the side of the parkway. He was not as prosperous-looking as George's specter had been; the man looked like an indigent or homeless person. The waving-arms signal attracted her attention and then, when she was only a few feet from the figure, it strode out in the road.

A startled Sylvia swerved to the left and spun the rear end of the Mustang out into the center lane. Luckily there was no other traffic there at the time. She came to a halt at a ninety-degree angle to the lane and quickly swung the car off the road to the right shoulder.

As George had done, and with a sense of absolute dread at the possibility that she had hit someone, Sylvia backed slowly along the service strip.

No man . . . no one . . . only the skid marks of her own tires.

At the next toll booth, Sylvia explained that she'd almost

hit a man on the road who might be a hobo. The toll collector smiled and nodded—knowingly, it seemed—but told her nothing.

The New Jersey State Police Barracks at Toms River has been reluctant to comment about accidents and reports of unusual things in the area. But that is understandable. With three hundred million cars traveling over five billion miles a year on the parkway, they have a great number of other things to be concerned about. But a former state trooper, who refused to be identified, confirmed that that stretch of parkway has more than its share of accidents.

Although the phantom seems to change his clothes, he doesn't change his spot—Exit 82. Prof. Snyder's research shows that the phantom averages five to six appearances a year, so the odds are fairly good that when you drive north-bound on the Garden State Parkway at night near Toms River, you might drive past one of the few ghosts known to haunt a superhighway.

# Juddville Is
# a State of Mind

In 1907, Jonas Dahlquist had the dubious honor of being the first person to be buried in the St. Paul cemetery near Juddville, Wisconsin. His grave is marked by a thin strip of concrete. His wife and two sons, Edward and Richard, now rest beside him. A single tombstone rests on the grave of Richard, a dwarf, who was probably the last of the Dahlquists.

The four graves are grouped together and are about sixty feet from the nearest plots. No other grave sites are similarly separated. In death, as in life, the Dahlquists remain reclusive.

Unincorporated Juddville, which Alan White (not his real name) calls a state of mind rather than a township, rests between Egg Harbor and Fish Creek. It was in a thick tangle of forest that Alan encountered the Dahlquists some thirty years after their deaths.

The White family has lived on the same land since 1898. Alan remembers the Dahlquists from his youth. Farmers in the area were poor, but the Dahlquists were poorer than poor.

Their farm was more hilly, more rocky, more swampy, and thus harder to farm than most.

Alan and his brother knew Richard Dahlquist. "With his corncob pipe and squeaky voice," Alan told reporter Gail Larson Toerpe, "he seemed like Popeye to us."

Besides being smaller than an average sixth grader, Richard had a club foot. Some of the children in the nearby school delighted in taunting him, but Alan and his brother did not—mostly because their dad "would have skinned us alive!" Perhaps as a result of their not ridiculing him, Richard was always pleasant to the brothers.

However, the Dahlquists *were* reclusive. No one knows why they stayed away from town. But Richard would occasionally hobble into the towns of Egg Harbor or Fish Creek. However, Richard had a bizarre quirk. He would start out toward one town, but if a car came along the road going the opposite way, Richard would turn around and follow it.

Alan had come across Richard many times and watched him totter down the wooded path from his house to the main road, where he would follow any car to either town.

Retired now, Alan often goes hunting. About five years ago on a dry November day, he walked, rifle in hand, into the tangled woods near the old Dahlquist house. Not actually planning to shoot anything, he went mainly for exercise.

All that's left of the Dahlquist home, in those woods and swamplands, are falling-down sides with a caved-in roof balanced on top. Alan had driven a ways into the forest down to a marshy area, dry at this time of year. Leaving his truck, he began to walk south toward a swamp near some old logging roads.

It had been a long time since he'd been there; though he couldn't see it, he knew he wasn't far from the remains of the Dahlquist house. As he remembered the poor family, he heard a strange piercing sound.

Alan thought it was a bird he'd never heard before. In a gravelly voice it seemed to call *"quick, quick."* The noise traveled through the barren trees from a hundred yards away.

Though the squawk was unsettling, Alan continued to walk up the hill toward the tumbledown house. He stopped not too far away to rest when he heard the noise for a third time.

Looking around, he heard it again from an evergreen thicket. The thicket was too dense for a bird large enough to make such a sound. Alan assumed some animal might be hidden nearby. So, although he was armed, he decided to walk down the hill to his truck.

As he walked, his thoughts turned to Richard. "Richard," Alan spoke out loud, "I know you had a hard life, but I want you to remember that my brother and I never made fun of you."

As he neared his truck, where he had first heard the sounds, Alan passed within twenty feet of a small lifeless tree. Suddenly from the tree the "creature" squawked very loudly. Alan looked up at the leafless tree and saw . . . nothing. It could not have hidden an animal of the size implied by the noise.

Then, coming from the cottonwood trees near the truck, there was another squawk. And on the road, near some cedars, came yet another. They all came in quick succession; nothing could have moved that fast. Curiosity overcame dread, and Alan walked toward a small cedar. Immediately the noise moved toward him, crying *"quick, quick."* He could hear it between himself and the tree. And then it screeched sharply right in front of him, near his feet.

He stared at the leaf-filled path beneath him and saw . . . nothing—no "thing." Stunned, he realized he was looking *through* the sound.

As he stood there dumbfounded, Alan felt a tap on his hip.

Swooping his arm backward to brush the thing away, he found nothing to brush.

Was it the ghosts of the Dahlquists? Alan turned around and walked toward the house. As he approached it, he heard the noise again, but this time it was far off, coming from a swampy area behind the house.

Not wanting to play tag with the invisible sounds, Alan went back to his truck. He could still hear the thing calling. Only now he wondered if instead of rasping "*quick, quick*" it wasn't calling " '*quist, 'quist. . . .*"

# The Greenville Ghost

It was a smallish two-story house in Greenville, Rhode Island. It had five rooms and a bathroom, a full basement, a porch, and gables on the second story. It wasn't your typical New England house, but it did have something that the other houses didn't—a ghost who liked to putter.

The house had been built in the 1920s by Arthur Roeger, a local carpenter and electrician, who lived there with his wife until his death in 1971. A year later, the house was sold to the Eagleson family and Arthur's widow moved to the West Coast to be with her daughter.

The Eaglesons—Duncan and Shirley and their two sons—found their new home full of peculiarities. Arthur had been an inveterate putterer and had approached the building and wiring of the house in his own eccentric style. In the basement stood a gasoline generator—power outages were no threat to this house—and often, when lightning storms struck, the Eaglesons were the only ones on the block with electricity.

The family soon discovered other oddities to the electrical system. Appliances would sometimes turn themselves on and off when no person was in the room. There were frequent, if momentary, brownouts. Although this strangeness provoked a raised eyebrow now and then, the Eaglesons thought that Arthur had just wired the house in his own inimitable fashion. They realized the wiring wasn't to blame when the footsteps began. . . .

At that time, Greenville was a small rural town; doors weren't locked and neighbors were welcome to visit. Most folks visiting the Eagleson house used the back entrance. That door opened onto a short hallway that led either to a door leading to the basement or to a short flight of steps leading to the kitchen door.

Although the kitchen was exceptionally large, anyone sitting in the kitchen could clearly hear visitors walking up the paved path to the back of the house. So the Eaglesons always knew they had a visitor before the person even rang or knocked.

But there were many times that they heard someone walking to the back door . . . who wasn't there. They heard the back door open and close and footsteps walking down the hall and up the steps. The doorknob on the kitchen door would rattle . . . but no one would come in. There would be silence. No one ever heard the sounds of someone walking away. And when one of the Eaglesons opened the door, the hall would be empty.

Other times, the Eaglesons would hear someone come in the back door, walk down the hall, and then go down the basement steps. They'd go into the basement to investigate, but the basement was always empty. And the hallway door was the only way out.

Eventually the Eaglesons realized that when the invisible visitor came to call, the electrical disturbances showed up as well. The ghostly footsteps would go down to the basement and the lights would flicker. There was no avoiding it: The

Eaglesons came to the inescapable conclusion that their invisible guest was the spirit of Arthur Roeger. Apparently the original owner of the house was too attached to it to let death interfere with his puttering around.

The family came to accept Arthur as a natural part of life in the house. He was not a malign spirit or a poltergeist. He never created a serious inconvenience, never really frightened anyone, and seemed entirely benign.

He was even helpful at times. One of the Eagleson boys had a record player that broke, and the young man could not fix it, though he tried. The record player was pushed to one side and sat in his room while the Eaglesons debated over fixing it or replacing it. One day the young man got the urge to try the record player one more time—and was startled to find it worked perfectly! The only answer was that Arthur had fixed it.

Duncan Eagleson passed away several years ago, and the boys have grown up and moved away. But Shirley is still there, undisturbed by the prospect of living alone in a haunted house. Yes, Arthur is still there, still puttering around.

To this day, when visitors hear the footsteps and the rattle of the doorknob and look up expecting to see someone enter, Shirley tells them, "Don't pay it any mind. It's just Arthur."

# My Name Is Dr. Z

I t was shortly after eight in the evening and Joel Martin was still in the WNYG radio station in Babylon, New York, where he was both news director and talk show host. Normally he would have left by this time, but tonight there was a mountain of papers and reels of audiotapes to go through for future programs.

At this hour, Martin was alone except for another broadcaster in the control room. From where Martin sat in his small office, the two men could not see each other unless one of them left the room he was in. For the next thirty minutes, Martin worked quietly at his desk. Suddenly he was interrupted by a man's voice behind him.

"Mr. Martin, how do you do?"

Startled, Martin spun around in his chair to see a frail-looking man, about sixty years old, with white hair. He was dressed conservatively, but his suit looked slightly large for him, giving him a rumpled appearance.

"What? Do I know you?" Martin asked.

"My name is Dr. Z," the man answered softly. "I was

74

interested in your radio programs about psychic phenomena. I'm pleased that you devote so much time to—how can I word it?—the supernatural.''

Martin nodded his acknowledgment. This was obviously an avid listener. The fact is that Martin did devote many of his weekly talk shows to every imaginable aspect of psychic and unexplained phenomena. Psychics and various experts on the paranormal were guests week after week as they explored, discussed, and debated. The programs had become popular in the Long Island, New York, area, where they were broadcast late in the evenings.

"Do you believe in the subjects you talk about?" the man asked.

"Well, I don't know," Martin admitted.

"That surprises me. You should take them seriously," the man said sternly, raising his hand and shaking a finger. "The work you're doing is important. Too many people lack knowledge about the psychic, the spiritual, and especially the world beyond."

"The world beyond?" Martin repeated.

"Yes. The spirit world. You do believe in life after death?" Dr. Z asked.

"I haven't thought about it," Martin confessed.

"Oh! I assumed you did because of the many programs you've done about life after death. Of course, there is no such thing as death."

"Well, I'm not a great believer in ghosts—"

The man interrupted. "We're talking about much more than that. We're talking about the importance of educating people that there is something beyond this plane. You know many people fear death. They have questions; they need help.

"It's important, even urgent, that you inform people of the certainty of a continuing existence beyond this one where the departed live on and where justice prevails even when it is so often denied on earth. You must continue to present such subjects, even in the face of those who scoff at the psychic—the so-called skeptics and debunkers. Even the religious zealots who would tell you the paranormal and mystical are 'the work of the devil.' You will face detractors in the years ahead. Don't be discouraged.''

Martin had not sought the stranger's advice, but he listened politely. There was something about Dr. Z that commanded attention, and Martin found it difficult to argue against him.

''How do you know all this?'' Martin asked.

Dr. Z fell silent.

''Are you a clergyman?''

There was no reply.

Before Martin could ask or say anything further, the stranger—who had preferred to stand the entire time—suddenly bid Martin good night. He turned slowly and walked out of the radio station into the chilly November night air. Poor weather, Martin observed, for a frail, elderly person who was not even wearing a coat.

Martin was more curious after the visit than he had been during it. For the encounter left a number of unanswered questions. For one thing, how did the man get into the locked radio station building? No one rang the night bell to enter. Could one of the doors have been inadvertently left open? More puzzling was how the man knew Martin was going to be in the building at that late hour. How did he instantly recognize Martin? What was the man a doctor of? He never said.

Perhaps Martin should have been more fearful. Yet he felt calmed by Dr. Z's message and the reassurance of the promise of life beyond death—even if he wasn't certain he believed everything he heard.

Martin soon pushed the unanswered questions to the back

of his mind. In fact, he said nothing further to anyone about the incident.

Several evenings later, Martin left WNYG with a colleague for a short drive to his home. As they drove out of the radio station's parking lot, Martin caught a glimpse of a figure in the beam of the car's headlights.

It looked like the man who called himself Dr. Z.

Martin turned his head quickly, but the figure he had seen only seconds before was gone.

He rubbed his forehead and eyes and thought, *I must be putting in too many hours—or these strange subjects I'm talking about are getting to me. The imagination sure can play tricks!*

Two days later, Martin left the station with his producer, Chris. As he drove away, he glanced in the car's rearview mirror.

"Oh, my God. You won't believe this," he told Chris. "Either I see a ghost in the rearview mirror or there's someone sitting in the backseat!"

"What?" Chris asked. Her head turned instantly. There was no one in the backseat.

"What did it look like?" Chris asked.

"It was a face. An older man. Thin and pale, as best as I could see. He was staring straight ahead," Martin answered.

"A phantom passenger?" Chris asked, smiling.

Martin slumped in his seat, not knowing what to make of the experience. He could not find the words to articulate his feelings. The incident was preposterous, even for a talk show host delving into the occult and supernatural.

Several days later, Martin and Chris were driving to a news assignment when suddenly Martin was startled to see Dr. Z standing on the street.

"It's him! I'm sure it is!" he exclaimed.

"Who? Where?" Chris asked. "I don't see anyone."

"The same face I saw in the rearview mirror and once before on the highway! Where did he go? He was here a moment ago!"

"Maybe you thought you saw him," Chris offered.

"Maybe my mind is running wild from too many shows about psychic phenomena," Martin declared. Deep inside, however, he felt certain it couldn't have been his imagination or a hallucination. Beyond that, he could offer no satisfactory explanation.

More than two weeks had passed since the first time Martin had met Dr. Z at the radio station. Again, he had all but put the unexplained experiences out of his mind, chalking them up to some temporary aberration.

It was shortly after nine P.M. It had been a long day. Martin had just finished recording some announcements for the next day's broadcast. He was just about to walk out of the recording studio when he was greeted by a familiar face and voice.

"Mr. Martin. Hello again."

It was Dr. Z. There was no mistake about it this time.

Martin was eager to ask all the questions that had gone through his mind since the first time he had met the stranger. He especially wished he could summon the courage to ask why he thought he saw the man several times outside of the radio station, on the street and in the rearview mirror.

But before Martin could utter a word, the man launched into the same discourse as during his first visit. This time, like the last, Martin felt powerless to interrupt as the stranger gently but firmly dominated the conversation.

And then abruptly the man stopped speaking. "It's time for me to leave," he said softly. Then he turned slowly to walk out of the building.

"Wait!" Martin ordered. The man stopped. "Where are you going?"

"Home," the man answered flatly.

"How? I don't know how you found your way in here again, but I hope you have a car outside. Do you?" Martin asked.

"No. I don't drive."

It was not a trivial question. For on Long Island there is little public transportation. Save for phoning ahead for a taxi (which the man had not done), there would be no way to travel except by automobile. There was no accessible transportation within miles of the radio station.

"How are you getting home, then?" Martin inquired. When the man did not answer, Martin offered to drive him home. "Do you live nearby?"

The man hesitated before answering. "Not too far." At Martin's insistence, Dr. Z agreed.

The two men walked out of the radio station. Once in the car, the stranger offered Martin directions. They drove for about fifteen minutes to the town of West Islip. During the ride, the man remained silent. Martin tried, but he could not engage his passenger in conversation. At the intersection of Union Boulevard and Gladstone Avenue, Dr. Z asked to get out. But Martin persuaded him to remain in the car so he could be driven right up to his house.

Martin turned onto Gladstone Avenue and stopped halfway up the block. Dr. Z got out of the car, thanked him, and added, "Remember, you must continue your programs. Good night, Mr. Martin."

Martin called after him. "Maybe you'd like to be a guest on a talk show sometime?" he asked half seriously.

Dr. Z continued walking, but he never walked into the front door of the house they had stopped at. Instead, the man walked down a dark path between two houses—and disappeared.

Martin shuddered at what he saw. Understandably, he remained bothered by the experience all that night and the next day. He had noted the address of the house Dr. Z had walked toward. So the next day Martin checked the local telephone directory. There was someone with that last name at that address! Now he could get to the bottom of this, he thought.

"Hello?" A woman answered Martin's phone call.

"Is Dr. Z in?" Martin asked politely. "My name is Joel Martin. I'm a local broadcaster. I spoke to Dr. Z just yesterday. When will he be home?"

"Is this a joke?" the woman's voice rose. "Dr. Z is dead. In fact, this week is a year that my husband is gone. He was murdered by one of his patients. My husband was a psychiatrist."

"Are you sure?" Martin asked. It was an obviously foolish question.

"Of course I'm sure!" And with those words the woman hung up the phone.

Martin sat stunned for a long time. Dr. Z did say there was a spirit world. Obviously he knew of what he spoke, since he was a spirit himself!

Had Dr. Z been a listener to Martin before he was killed? And was he still listening from somewhere in the world beyond?

# The Haunted House of Brown's Flat

On a lonely hill outside the New Brunswick farming community of Brown's Flat lies the ruin of a haunted house. Built in 1870, the old farmhouse commands a spectacular view of the Saint John River and the village, spread out along both sides of the road.

The Andrews family—Eva, Michael, and their two daughters, Lee and Petra—moved into the house in 1948, after Michael landed a job as a mechanic in the Brown's Flat garage. They fell in love with their new home at first sight. Like many New Brunswick houses of that era, it was a two-story white clapboard structure, with a peaked roof and single dormer window. The floorboards in the kitchen, hewn from maple logs, were up to eighteen inches wide. A massive carved oak staircase ran up the center of the house. There had originally been two great fireplaces, one in the living room and one in the kitchen, but an earlier tenant had walled these up when woodstoves became commonplace. The back kitchen overlooked an expanse of pasture stretching down to the river road. It was a lonely but majestic place.

It was also haunted.

The Andrewses' first hint that they might be sharing their residence with spirits came on a beautiful August morning shortly after they moved in. Two-year-old Lee was playing on the kitchen floor while her mother made breakfast for the family. It was a peaceful domestic scene, with the sun streaming in the windows and the smell of porridge and coffee thick in the air. Suddenly the tranquility was shattered by the earsplitting sound of a bell.

Eva Andrews was so startled that she dropped a bowl of porridge. Both Lee and her five-year-old sister, Petra, clapped their hands over their ears, and the dog began to howl. Eva wondered if she was hearing things until she saw the children and realized they heard it, too.

The clamor continued for thirty seconds—long enough for Eva to run through the house, looking out all the windows and both doors in an attempt to find the unseen bell. She thought some prankster might be outside, jangling a cowbell—but there wasn't a soul in sight. With the bright sunshine and short-cropped grass, they couldn't possibly have hidden—apart from which, the sound appeared to be coming from within the house itself! Baffled, Eva returned to the kitchen. As she rejoined her children, the ringing stopped.

Eva Andrews was a veteran of the Canadian Women's Army Corps; she was not easily frightened. It never even occurred to her to move out. But then, the ghosts weren't finished yet. . . .

August gave way to September, then October; the air grew crisp, and across the hills the foliage blazed with autumn colors. Michael Andrews took to bringing in armloads of wood for the stove before going to work. One mid-October evening he had gone to work the night shift—eleven P.M. to seven A.M. Eva saw him off, then tucked the children in, removed the final pan of cookies from the oven, and banked the fires before going upstairs to her bedroom. The old staircase creaked with every step as she ascended. She had just climbed into bed and turned off the lights when she heard the front door open.

Her first thought was that it must be Michael, returning for some item he had forgotten. She called his name, but no one answered. This was odd, as the front door had been locked, yet had opened effortlessly—only her husband had a key. She called again, more urgently; still no answer. Then she heard the door close, and footsteps started up the stairs. As always, the steps creaked and groaned with every footfall.

Eva Andrews was terrified. Here she was, alone on a remote hilltop in the middle of the night, with two small children and no gun, and someone was slowly and deliberately climbing the stairs toward her room! She did the only thing she could: She froze. Every hair on her body stood on end. Scarcely breathing, she waited for the inevitable moment.

The footsteps cleared the stairs and turned toward the bedroom. Just as they reached the door, Eva screamed . . . and the footsteps stopped.

Eva crouched in her bed for half an hour before rallying the nerve to get up and turn on the lights. Armed with a bread knife, she searched the whole house—and found no one.

The haunting was repeated every night for the next two weeks. At the end of that time, Eva was a nervous wreck. In desperation, she finally called her mother, Geraldine Morgan.

Geraldine was an eminently sensible lady. She volunteered to come visit for a week and assess the situation. Upon her arrival, she promptly searched the house, then checked the lock on the front door, and found nothing out of the ordinary. That evening she made certain that she was the last person up the stairs—and as she went up, she sprinkled the steps behind her with flour. The family settled down to await the ghostly footsteps, but the footsteps never came. In fact, they were never heard again.

The hauntings, however, continued. There was one room in the old house that no one could sleep in because of the noises—they sounded like chains or, as Geraldine put it, "someone rattling a wire inside a stovepipe." In fact, that was exactly what Geraldine believed it to be—an old piece of wire rattling around in one of the abandoned chimneys.

The night after she dusted the steps with flour, Geraldine volunteered to sleep in the "haunted" room, claiming that no noise had ever kept her awake in the past. No sooner had she climbed into bed than the cacophony began. Contrary to previous statements, it did *not* sound like wires—it was definitely a chain, and it grew progressively louder.

Geraldine clenched her teeth, determined to ride it out. The sweat sprang out on her forehead, and her breathing grew labored. Suddenly she felt something yank the sheets down off her chest. Annoyed, she grabbed them and pulled them back up—only to have them pulled off again from the *foot* of the bed! She tried to reach for them . . . and a pressure like an anvil descended on her chest. The chain-rattling grew louder, and the pressure increased until she could hardly breathe. Although she struggled to sit up, she found herself pinned to the bed. The weight was crushing her. With a final desperate effort, she rolled off the bed, crawled to the door, and flung it open.

No one ever tried to sleep in that room again. Eva made up a bed for her mother in the children's bedroom. *That* room had a quirk of its own, albeit a benign one: No matter how much noise the children made inside, nothing could be heard in the hall. Even with your ear to the door, the room was silent as a tomb.

The Andrews family stayed in the old house all winter, but

the hauntings never stopped. There were always windows banging shut and doors creaking open. And an invisible someone rocked in the old rocking chair in the kitchen until the day they left.

The Andrews family moved out in the spring of 1949. The house stayed vacant—maybe the locals knew more about the house than they let on.

In 1955, the Canadian Armed Forces moved to a base just a few miles away, taking over a large tract of land—and the old farmhouse now sat on their artillery range! The army took to using the old house as a target. As a result, in 1963, when Lee Andrews returned to Brown's Flat for a visit, though the frame of the house remained, the roof had fallen in.

Still, the ghosts may not have left. Artillery shells have no effect on the dead.

# The Unfriendly House on Old Homestead Road

*I*n 1981, the Grant family moved into their new home on
Old Homestead Road in St. Charles, Illinois. It was a
large ranch house on a few acres of land and was rather
isolated. Hal Grant, his wife Marilyn, and their small daughter Jill (not their real names) had no idea they were moving
into a house that did not want them.

The house was less than a dozen years old. It had three
bedrooms, a large kitchen, a den, and patio doors that opened
to the backyard. The house had no attic and the basement was
an unfinished crawl space.

Behind the house was a small barn, where the Grants decided to keep a few farm animals and their menagerie. The
Grants had a cat, a dog, parakeets, canaries, and fish, all of
which Jill helped care for.

One day Marilyn was home alone taking a bath when she
heard strange footsteps coming down the hallway. The dog
was tied up outside, nor had it barked or made any sounds.
Worried, Marilyn got out of the tub and checked the house.
No one was there. At other times, Hal also heard footsteps.

But when he went to look, he could find no one was ever there, either.

Marilyn once was in the kitchen preparing dinner when she heard music. No one had on the stereo or radios, and she had no idea where it was coming from. She asked Hal to come into the kitchen to listen, but he heard nothing. When she hummed the tune for him, he recognized it as Scottish music because he had marched to it in the army.

Sometimes they would hear a loud bang in one of the bedrooms. Marilyn and Hal would go in the room thinking something had fallen, but things in the room would be undisturbed. The loud bangs would move from one bedroom to another, but the Grants never found anything broken or disturbed. Sometimes lights would turn themselves on and off, windows and doors would open.

Approximately six months after moving in, Marilyn Grant starting having recurring nightmares. They were pretty horrible: She usually dreamed she and her daughter were dead, either stabbed and mutilated . . . or eaten.

Soon Jill was telling her mother that spirits were floating around in her bedroom. Eventually Jill hung a crucifix over her bed, so she could sleep undisturbed. Since Marilyn refused to let Jill watch scary movies or read horror stories, she had no idea where Jill had gotten this notion. As time went by, Jill, who was around seven at the time, felt the crucifix wasn't enough and convinced her grandmother to bring her a bottle of holy water.

Jill also told Marilyn her grandfather had come to visit one night. She described Marilyn's grandfather quite well, which threw Marilyn into a panic, since her grandfather had died more than twenty years before and there were no pictures of him.

One weekend her brother came to visit and stayed for the night. He was given the spare bedroom. Marilyn had no idea anything was wrong until breakfast, when her brother announced that he'd been awakened at two A.M. by invisible hands shaking the bed.

Another time, her mother and father came to visit. Marilyn's father was tired from playing with Jill and he went to the spare bedroom to take a nap. A short while later he came out of the bedroom.

"Okay, let's go," he told his wife.

"Why?" Marilyn's mother was not ready to leave.

"You just told me to. You shook my arm and said, 'Let's go.' "

"I did not. I've been in this room the entire time!"

The first time Marilyn finally saw the ghost herself, she'd been home sick. Unable to sleep one night, she got out of bed and went into the hallway. She felt the hallway grow very cold. At first she thought it was because she was ill . . . but a white misty form coalesced in the hall and floated toward her. She did not wait around to see where it went.

Hal was asleep at the time and saw nothing. Marilyn saw the white mist again and again, but it was always when Hal was asleep. It seemed that most of the paranormal activity occurred around Marilyn.

As time went by, all their small farm animals and pets began dying off. The birds went first, followed by the chickens and rabbits. Marilyn had bad dreams about the cat. It later died.

Unable to pretend that things in the house were normal, Marilyn consulted a psychic. She picked a name out of the phone book and went to see a Madame Mary. Marilyn only said she had a problem—not what the problem was—but Madame Mary announced to Marilyn that her house was not only cursed but it didn't like her. And under no circumstances was Marilyn to go into the basement.

Suddenly Marilyn realized that both their cat and dog, who

roamed the house and yard freely, refused to go into the basement. When she went back home and told her husband about the psychic, they had a terrible argument over it—even though Hal knew strange things were going on in the house and had no idea what to do about it.

The Grants' arguments escalated. One evening they had a screaming battle. Marilyn became so enraged she picked up the telephone and threw it at Hal. It missed and went through a plate-glass window, shattering it. Marilyn was so upset she ran crying from the room. Hal followed her; when they returned, somehow the plate-glass window was put back together—and there was no shattered glass anywhere!

By now the Grants' marriage was cracking under the strain. Marilyn felt something evil was after her. She packed up and left, taking their daughter. Hal stayed in the house by himself; the terrifying phenomena calmed down, but it still continued—as it had for more than two years.

With nowhere to turn, the Grants decided they needed help from experts. They agreed to have a group of investigators interview them and examine the house. They were John Preston (not his real name), a psychic who had a television show at the time; Norman Basile, a ghost hunter in the Chicago area; and Jean Lord (not her real name), another psychic who used psychometry (perceiving information by touching an object or area). Added to the group was a television cameraman.

So in the late summer of 1983, everyone met at the "cursed" house. Hal Grant was still living there alone; Marilyn arrived at the house for the interviews. They all also toured the grounds and the four ghost hunters were surprised to find an Indian burial mound not far away!

After the interviews, the Grants left the intrepid ghost hunters to fend for themselves—because the ghost hunters were going to stay the night.

In addition to the video camera, they all had various cameras of their own. Jean Lord brought a Polaroid camera and immediately took pictures outside the house. The instantly developed pictures all had unusual streaks of light on them. Jean was afraid the camera was defective, but it worked normally when they were in the house.

Norman Basile used infrared film. When it was later developed, it too had unusual lights on the film—as well as faces appearing in the front window.

The group decided to separate; each person would walk through the house and record his or her individual impressions. They would meet later in the den and compare notes, which would be recorded on camera for a future television show.

All of them agreed there was a very negative feeling in the guest bedroom. Jean Lord lay down on the bed there and felt the bed shake beneath her.

John Preston felt fear in the basement. He meditated and eventually saw three white forms appear there, but the feeling he got was one of friendliness.

Norman Basile felt a coldness in the living room. When he opened the basement door for the first time, he smelled a pungent, rotting odor, which he felt was not normal. He also heard strange crackling noises.

The general consensus was that the house had a very strong energy to it. The ghost hunters recalled something the Grants said: Hal had once seen lightning crawling along the ground! And Marilyn's brother once described the underground electrical wires leading to an outdoor lamp as "burning up under the ground."

Was a negative energy sucking out the life force of the animals and people? Possibly. Were the spirits those of Indians centered on the burial mound? Probably. Did the house not want the Grants? Definitely.

Preston suggested an appeasement ritual for the Indian ghosts. Oils, incense, and candles were scattered around the house. All the doors and windows were opened to allow the spirits to move freely. Four metal rods were hammered into the ground not far from the house. Each person stood at one of the rods; suddenly Norman Basile could see a huge number of ghostly figures watching. A hole was dug in the center and salt and corn were buried as gifts to the spirits. John Preston called out for a sign that the bargain had been made and was answered with an Indian whoop.

Hal Grant was instructed not to touch anything until he sold the house and moved. At that time, he was to pull up the stakes to release the spirits. A few weeks later, a curious Grant walked into the staked area and poked around—that night, invisible hands shook his bed and ripped off the covers! After that, Grant stayed out of the area.

The house was up for sale for a long time. One day a woman interested in the house was walking through it with Hal Grant. When they reached the master bedroom, suddenly the window blinds pulled themselves up with a snap—as though invisible hands had yanked on them! Obviously the ghosts were not pleased with the prospective buyer, who left in a panic.

Another family now lives in the house on Old Homestead Road. We can only hope the house likes them.

# Bigfoot Central

Cliff Crook's fascination with the creature known as Bigfoot began in 1956 when he ran into one himself. As a teenager, Cliff and several friends had gone camping in a wild and untamed area located between Woodinville and Duvall in the state of Washington.

The friends had set up a campsite in a wooded section not far from a swamp. After pitching the tents and setting up all their gear, they built a cozy campfire. The boys sat around the fire chatting, eating, and drinking soda into the night.

Cliff remembers that sometime around midnight they heard strange sounds coming from the swamp—sounds like someone very large and bulky was walking toward them. The steps came to a halt about twelve feet from their camp. Since it was dark and they were surrounded by seven-foot-tall underbrush, the boys couldn't see a thing.

But the dog they had brought with them started barking. And from the dark bushes came answering sounds that Cliff can only describe as *"arr-garr, larr-garr."*

The dog rushed into the bushes. The boys heard the sounds

of a struggle—and then the dog was thrown out of the bushes and back into the campsite. Looming up over the tall underbrush was a huge dark form. It shambled after the dog, and by the light of the fire the boys could see a tall, hairy humanoid beast—Bigfoot!

When it looked as though the creature was about to join the boys around the campfire, Cliff pulled a hot stick out of the fire and pitched it at the beast. It let out a horrendous roar. The creature took off back to the swamp, and Cliff and his friends ran in the opposite direction.

Barefoot, they fled through the darkness to Cliff's father's house. Mr. Crook was less than pleased to be awakened in the middle of the night and be told an unbelievable story. He was even unhappier to find out the frightened boys had fled their campsite, leaving all their equipment behind. He was so angry, he wouldn't let them in the house and made them sleep outside on the ground.

Cliff was in for even more unpleasantness. No one in town believed the incredible story about the strange creature, much less his parents. Younger kids were forbidden to play with him, lest he frighten them with weird tales. Cliff decided the solution was to find out where the creature lived. Then he would get the townspeople to follow him to the creature's lair and show it to them, as proof he was not making up the story. And Cliff Crook has been looking for Bigfoot ever since.

He never did find that Bigfoot, but he has found others. His home in Bothell, Washington, now houses a small museum filled with evidence of Bigfoot. In a display case is a sample of Bigfoot hair. There are photos and videotapes of Bigfoot taken from all over the world. One wall is covered with maps which pinpoint Bigfoot sightings. Another wall is covered with hundreds of books written over the years by scientists and investigators alike.

The museum also houses an impressive collection of plaster

casts of Bigfoot footprints. Two of the more recent castings are of seven-by-fifteen-inch footprints of a heavily callused humanlike foot (toes, but no claws). The footprints were found in a sandbar by the upper Nisqually River in Pierce County, Washington.

Another recent plaster cast of a footprint was made by Cliff after he received a call from three people who were picking mushrooms in Mt. Rainier National Park. The mushroom hunters heard odd noises—and smelled something atrocious—in the nearby woods. On the same day, an actual siting was reported just a few miles away.

Cliff flew to the site and found not only clear footprints but evidence that something had blazed a trail away from the mushroom pickers and toward the reported siting. He took a plaster cast of an exceptionally clear footprint, which was fourteen inches long, seven inches wide at the toe, and went three inches deep into the hardened soil.

The depth of the impression led Cliff to believe the creature weighed more than 450 pounds. The stride (distance between the footprints) was almost 37 inches, which meant the creature was about seven and a half feet tall. The stride was twice that of an ordinary man.

In 1982, Cliff Crook started Bigfoot Central, the official Bigfoot/Sasquatch report center and data base for North America. It is an information clearinghouse and in 1991 it also became a nonprofit foundation for the preservation of the Sasquatch.

Bigfoot Central has collected and researched thousands of sightings, not just in the Pacific Northwest. However, the Pacific Northwest is a traditional location for Bigfoot. Since 1988, there have been close to six hundred sightings in the western United States, including more than two hundred in the state of Washington.

Native Americans in the Pacific Northwest have several

names for this huge manlike creature, and the commonly used term *Sasquatch* derives from Indian words meaning "wild man of the woods." The average Bigfoot is approximately seven and a half feet tall. It is bipedal (it walks upright) and is covered with dark hair, usually brown or black, but sometimes beige. It is broad-shouldered, short-necked, with a flat face and sloping forehead.

There are many reasons why further evidence of Bigfoot's existence has not been found. No hunter has ever killed one. No one has ever found the remains of a body. It is likely that there are very few such creatures left, perhaps no more than a few hundred; they go deeper into the inaccessible areas of nature as civilization encroaches. They may take care of each other, so that if one is sick or injured, it is rescued and spirited away. Cliff Crook speculates that they may bury their dead in a hidden location, like the legendary elephant burial ground. Also, they are solitary, generally nocturnal, highly intelligent, and very fast.

Cliff believes that the creatures are not dangerous and need to be protected legally. Bigfoot Central has been lobbying for such legislation. Skamania County, Washington, passed an ordinance making it a felony for "any premeditated, willful and wanton slaying of any such creature." It provides for a $10,000 fine and/or jail for up to five years.

Cliff also helped organized the first Bigfoot festival. It is held annually in the town of Baker, Washington. One of the first guests was "Harry," the giant and gentle Bigfoot from the movie and television show, *Harry and the Hendersons*.

So if you have seen or heard a Bigfoot or want to find out more about Cliff Crook's work, order the center's newsletter, or get information about the next festival, call 1-800-83-BIGFOOT.

# Mrs. Ackley's Ghosts

Hauntings rarely get much national press coverage these days, but when money is involved, the rules change. In March 1990, national television reported that strange things were happening in Nyack, a suburban community north of New York City. Newspapers across the country were also covering this most unusual story. It seems that one Jeffrey Stambovsky petitioned the court for a refund of his $32,000, which had been a down payment on a $650,000 Victorian waterfront home. Stambovsky, a Wall Street broker, had just discovered from his local architect that the house was haunted.

Stambovsky approached the owner, Helen Ackley, with this startling information, only to find that she already knew about it. In fact, she verified that the house at 1 Leveta Place was haunted not by one but by at least *three* spirits from the other side: a young woman wearing a hooded cape, a young naval officer, and an old man with white hair.

Since ghosts were not part of his family plan, Stambovsky wanted his money back. Mrs. Ackley refused, and they ended up in court. Apparently the judge also agreed with Mrs. Ackley, ruling that spirits were not a good enough reason to back out of a contract. Fearing for his wife and child, Stambovsky walked away from both his deposit and the house.

As a result, the Ackleys were besieged by reporters. Perhaps all this publicity would help find a buyer; soon the house was back on the market again. In fact, the local real estate office received many calls about the house, but none of them seemed serious—especially the one call from a patient in a mental hospital.

The media coverage attracted the interest of the Amazing Kreskin, one of the world's leading "mentalists." Kreskin was looking for a large house as a possible receptacle for his huge collection of memorabilia, and he preferred a haunted house, of course.

Kreskin had been looking at other possible haunted houses. One, in Eddyville, New York, supposedly shook and vibrated at night. Kreskin easily found a nearby willow tree had been the culprit, rubbing its branches against the roof. Another home supposedly made crashing noises at night. That turned out to be a bartender at the local pub, throwing out his glass bottles at night.

Kreskin stayed overnight at the Nyack house that spring. Later he made the announcement that indeed the house was haunted. He'd seen objects move about the house by an unseen hand. And one of his experiments had been to order the ghost to knock down a piece of wood. The ghost gladly obliged.

This positive affirmation pleased Mrs. Ackley. She'd been telling the truth all along.

Helen and George Ackley and their children moved from their Maryland farm to the Nyack house in 1967. They had no idea about the haunted condition of the house until some local children approached them and told the family about the spooky legends.

Helen dismissed them as rumors until things around the house started moving by themselves. Lamps would sway back and forth, the French doors would swing open, windows would fling themselves shut. Friends were skeptical until they, too, saw the strange things happen.

At the same time, Mrs. Ackley and her children felt the presence of some unseen beings in the house. Her daughter often felt that she shared her bedroom with an invisible roommate.

The ghosts were never seen until the Ackleys started major renovations to the old home. Perhaps the ghosts were disturbed by the noise and workmen, or by changes to the home.

One day Mrs. Ackley was in the living room painting a wall. She felt something was in the room with her. She turned her head and saw a cheerful old man with white hair and red cheeks sitting in midair, staring at her.

"Do you approve?" she asked, gesturing at the paint.

The ethereal spirit smiled and nodded his approval, still smiling as he faded away.

Another time, a visiting relative who was staying overnight woke before daylight. She heard someone walking around the house and soon a man dressed in a Revolutionary War uniform walked into her room. He sat on her bed and proceeded to open a book and read it. He seemed to be looking for something. After a few minutes his search ended, he closed the book, and he walked out of the room, leaving the shocked relative still in bed.

This spirit was different than the other ghost the family often saw. Most commonly they saw a more casual ghost who often wore comfortable moccasins and was usually seen walking up the basement stairs.

Another ghost was a young woman in her twenties who usually wore a hooded cape.

Helen Ackley wrote an account of the family's adventures with the three ghosts, which appeared in a 1977 issue of *Reader's Digest*. She said the spirits were not evil but benign, and she offered the following examples:

• The ghosts would wake the children up in the morning so they wouldn't be late for school. The ghosts appeared more to the children to the adults.

• The ghosts most definitely took the Ackley family under their wings, so to speak. Occasionally a ghost would leave them gifts. A pair of silver tongs were left for daughter Cynthia when she got married. A small, embossed gold ring was left when the Ackleys' first grandchild was born.

All attempts to find the origin of these objects were made, but the family was never able to explain these "gifts from beyond." Nor have the Ackleys or anyone else, been able to find out the identities of the three spirits.

Mrs. Ackley was worried that, although she had plenty of company in that house, she might not find another buyer for it. Eventually the Nyack house did sell, presumably to someone who doesn't think three's a crowd. . . .

Since this story was written, the Nyack house was in the newspapers once more. An appeals court ruled that "as a matter of law" the house *was* haunted. This allowed Jeffrey Stambovsky to file suit to recover the down payment they had lost, making them the first people ever to sue for "ectoplasmic fraud."

# There Are More Than Spies at Spy House

Thomas Whitlock acquired land from local Indians in the Bayshore area and built his house in 1663. It was the first house built on the New Jersey shore.

Whitlock placed the house at the center of his property, which he called Shoal Harbor Plantation, and proceeded to develop a thriving business that led to the expansion of the house. It was used variously as a private dwelling, farmhouse, tavern, and den of Revolutionary War spies over the ensuing 230 years.

Spy House earned its nickname and garnered its first spiritual visitors at the time of the Revolutionary War. It was between 1779 and 1783 that the Seabrook family, descendants of the Whitlocks, lived in the house and farmed locally. But by this time, the orchards and farmlands that had bordered the rear of the house had been taken over by the sea. The "plantation" was gone and the house had to find another way to sustain itself.

Mrs. Seabrook, in the face of a British occupation of Monmouth County—and an alarming number of Tories in the county—turned the house into an inn to preserve it from being destroyed by the British.

There were few other inns in the Bayshore area, and rather than burn it, The British commander decided to patronize it. This was a matter of convenience more than anything else, as the British brought supplies ashore in the shallows of the Bayshore area, only a few miles from Sandy Hook. The landing point was adjacent to Spy House and the location was perfect as a stop for General Howe's troops—a place to rest and dine.

It was at this point that a tradition of espionage began at Spy House.

In 1779, General George Washington created a commission for a Colonel John Stillwell, who inhabited a "coast watcher" position at nearby Garret Hill. For more than five years, he managed to chronicle all of the arrivals and departures of British shipping through the narrows. He logged the supplies as well as guns as they arrived, and passed this information on to the privateers who frequented Spy House. They, in turn, planned and carried out raids on British ships as soon as they cleared Sandy Hook. Thirty-nine successful raids depleted British supplies and forced them to slow their pursuit of Washington through New Jersey and into Pennsylvania.

Suspecting that the privateers had something to do with the raids, the British set the house on fire. They also destroyed the water buckets so that the fire could not be put out after they left. When they set the house afire, they neglected to discover the false closet, staircases, and the long escape tunnel full of rebel contraband bound for Washington's storehouses. A rebel soldier and a young spy/barmaid were caught and either suffocated in the smoke or were crushed by a collapse of the tunnel ceiling.

They are still there . . . in the tunnel. People see a pretty girl wearing a lovely pink and green dress, hovering in fear at the edge of the tunnel. Sometimes she waits at the front door of Spy House, apparently for the arrival of the soldier who had died with her.

According to Spy House curator, Mrs. Gertrude Neidlinger, the house is alive with the dead. There are more than twenty-seven identified spirits in residence (in the house and outbuildings) nearly all the time, and there are others who seem to appear at irregular times and different places. Many have been identified by name and others by the locations on the property that they frequent.

There is a young boy named Peter who likes to amuse himself by moving parts of the antique sewing machines in one of the rooms. Occasionally unsuspecting visitors are unnerved when a piece of equipment seems to move when no one is near it.

Abigail, a very well dressed young woman in her mid-thirties, sits by the east window looking off in the distance. She has a handkerchief in her hand and is weeping. She has been seen and contacted by psychics who have attempted but failed to determine the nature of her grief. Others who have seen her have testified that she did not notice them at all. She just looks from the window and cries.

Seen only a few feet from Abigail is a male ghost who is, strangely enough, only visible from the knees down. (Partial apparitions were also spoken of by paranormal expert Dr. Hans Holzer. He documented the case of the "catacomb ghosts"—monks who were seen to walk in ranks as if on the way to vespers in the Roman catacombs. Their robed forms were only seen from about the knees up. Investigation into the archaeological substrata of the catacombs disclosed that the original path was some eighteen inches to two feet lower than the current path. The monks were simply walking on the path that they knew . . . the one that was there at the time they died.)

This bodyless set of male legs, which is utterly unidentifiable, is occasionally known to pinch stout female visitors—a large number of women (the number ranges between thirty and forty) have reported being pinched. Slender females are apparently immune. Otherwise, he is harmless.

Visitors, especially those who come to the museum simply to get a good evening view of Raritan Bay, report hearing the sounds of two children playing inside the house. Their voices are heard laughing at a number of household locations and seem to move while they are being heard—as if the children themselves are running through the house.

The sounds of playing children are also heard in the backyard of the house—the part that edges the water. History and local folklore records that the water's edge once was the entrance to an orchard, before the sea washed it away. Children liked to climb the trees there and gather up the sweet pears and apples to eat.

In addition to things being mysteriously rearranged, there is the constant hiding of things at Spy House. Ms. Neidlinger has reported the frequent disappearance of wool that had been on the spinning looms in the museum. As all of the artifacts in the museum are totally open to the public and are "hands-on," there is a chance that the missing wool might have been snitched by the visitors. The explanation is plausible but not probable when matched up with the frequency of the accounts. In addition, in many of the cases the wool is found in other spots around the house. It is crammed into bureau drawers (always in the same back right-hand corner) and jammed into crevices of the secret closets and passages—places where a tourist might never look. The consistency of this "squirreling away" of the wool points to a paranormal rather than a natural explanation.

A number of the artifacts shift positions as well. Nothing in the museum is locked up; everything is placed where it would be in normal everyday use. Perhaps the ghostly inhabitants find this pleasing, even comforting—the ghosts may need to move and hide artifacts in order to feel secure.

This possibility is more than conjecture. Ghost researchers in the latter half of this century have hypothesized that a ghost is lost both in time and space. It retains a remembered physical identity and is connected to either a specific location or a compelling though uncompleted action. Since the histories of most of the Spy House ghosts are not known, questions about their actions cannot be answered. But Spy House—with its restored authenticity and historical artifacts—certainly serves as a familiar and comforting location for former inhabitants, guests at the inn, and Revolutionary spies.

The overall atmosphere of Spy House is warm and, a number of visiting psychics say, conducive to the current and future appearance of spiritual visitors.

Spy House, also known as the Whitlock-Seabrook House, is located in Port Monmouth, New Jersey, off exit 117 of the Garden State Parkway. It is open Saturdays from one to three-thirty P.M. and Sundays from two-twenty to five P.M. Admission is free, but there is always a need for donations—which, of course, would help maintain a home for the ghosts.

# The Story of Delphin Rambert

Patrick Pierre McCurdy, an American living in Virginia, had in his possession various papers—letters, memoirs, family history—assembled by his French uncle, Jacques Hillairet de Boisferon. Most of the information in these documents was already familiar to Patrick, who always had a high regard for his mother's only brother—a hero of both world wars and an exceptionally courageous man.

Jacques was born on July 18, 1898 in Périers, France, a small town in Normandy some forty miles south of Cherbourg. In 1900, when Jacques was a very young child, he moved with his family to Angers, on the Loire River, where he grew up. He served in the French army from 1916 to 1919 and fought in the Battle of Verdun, for which he received the Croix de Guerre with the bronze star, France's highest honor for bravery.

During World War II he served in the French Resistance, escaping in 1942 to join the Free French Forces in Algeria. He made his way back to France through the military campaigns in Italy.

In civilian life, Jacques was an electrical engineer. He was also an amateur pilot, logging over five thousand hours in the air. He married late in life, at age seventy, to a woman with whom he had been in love for many years—the widow of his best friend.

Jacques Hillairet de Boisferon presented a very striking figure, not only because of his imposing height—well over six feet—but because of his completely shaven head. This unusual practice stemmed from those horrific months in the trenches of Verdun when shaving one's head was the best and perhaps only way to avoid lice.

Possibly because of all his war experiences, Jacques was an utterly pragmatic man throughout his life. So it was with increasing fascination that Patrick McCurdy came across and read Jacques's account of a very curious incident. . . .

Jacques's own uncle, Bernard de Boisferon, had spent his last years living in a small house in Saint-Ciers-sur-Gironde, a town about thirty-five miles north of Bordeaux in the south of France. On receiving a telegram with the news of his uncle's death in 1923, Jacques boarded an overnight train to Saint-Ciers and arrived there the next morning.

Jacques had not been to Saint-Ciers since he was two years old in 1900, and knew nothing of the town or its inhabitants. He immediately checked into a room at the small hotel of Saint-Ciers, then proceeded to his uncle's house.

The day was taken up with the usual sad formalities. A few neighbors paid their respects, but the hours went by very slowly.

Night fell. Jacques sat up until midnight, watching over the bier of his uncle. Then it was the turn of Bernard's old servant to continue the vigil, and Jacques was free to walk back to the hotel. He looked forward to catching a few hours of sleep.

It was a dark night with a fine drizzle. As he crossed the small garden between the front steps of his uncle's house and the gate, Jacques heard footsteps. He paused at the edge of the road. Coming toward him, headed in the direction of the town, was an old, rather small man with a white mustache. But the most striking characteristic about him was the peculiar way he walked: stiffly, legs apart.

The old man looked up at Jacques. "Ah, so poor Monsieur de Boisferon has passed away."

Since they were walking in the same direction, they naturally decided to keep each other company.

"Who are you?" the old man asked as they walked.

"I am Bernard de Boisferon's nephew. His brother René was my father."

The old man smiled. "I knew your father well. I knew your grandfather Pierre. As a matter of fact, I also knew your great-grandfather! I remember he wore his hair in a queue and dressed in the old-fashioned clothes of his younger years."

He was referring to Jean-François Hillairet de Boisferon, who had lived from 1789 to 1879. The old man went on to relate various tidbits about this eccentric ancestor of Jacques's. Apparently, even at his advanced age, Jean-François had a way with women and was known in Saint-Ciers an an incorrigible flirt. He was quite a contrast to his son Pierre, upstanding lawyer, the town's mayor, and apparently a rather stern fellow.

Jacques, who had known nothing of his great-grandfather, was charmed by the old man's tales of a time long past and mentally stored away the information. When they reached Saint-Ciers, Jacques offered his hand to the old man and mentioned he was headed for the hotel.

"Ah, yes, the hotel," the old man said. "My sister is Madame Chaumet, the wife of the owner. She runs the place. My name, by the way, is Delphin Rambert."

With that, the two men parted. The next day Jacques buried his uncle, then left town. Instead of going directly home, he stopped to see his mother in Angiers to let her know the details of Uncle Bernard's funeral. In the course of his visit, he told her about Delphin Rambert, who had much to say about Jacques's great-grandfather.

As Jacques related Rambert's description of an old roue, his mother smiled and confirmed that Jean-François's antics caused a lot of family gossip.

Three weeks later, legal matters brought Jacques to Saint-Ciers once again. This time Bernard's forty-five-year-old son Pierre met him at the train station.

They breakfasted at the Hotel Chaumet. Their meal was served by Madame Chaumet herself. Jacques introduced himself to the kind woman and mentioned he had met her brother, Delphin Rambert, three weeks before.

"That's impossible!" she said, shocked. "My brother is dead!"

"In the three weeks since I saw him? I'm so sorry."

"What are you talking about?" she demanded. "My brother's been dead for four years."

Jacques was incredulous. Surely Madame Chaumet was playing a joke on an innocent stranger—a joke he did not find particularly funny.

To prove her point, Madame Chaumet showed her two guests various papers, certificates, and so forth. The facts were indisputable: Delphin Rambert had died in 1919 at the age of sixty-four.

Yet when Jacques described the man who had accompanied him back to town that dark night, Madame Chaumet nodded with recognition. Her brother had looked exactly like that, she said. Moreover, her brother had suffered from prostate problems that made walking difficult—the stiff-legged gait! As for the amusing stories about Jacques's ancestors, Madame Chaumet confirmed that her brother, who had been much older than she, would have been able to remember them.

Through the years, Jacques often recounted his meeting with Delphin Rambert. He would go over and over it in his mind, looking for a rational explanation. Could he have been so affected by his uncle's death that he hallucinated the entire encounter? But he'd scarcely known his uncle. More importantly, could he have hallucinated so accurately about a man he never knew existed?

Did an imposter assume the identity of a long-dead man? It made no sense that someone would go to such great lengths for an elaborate hoax—and for what purpose? Neither Jacques nor Pierre nor Madame Chaumet could come up with a single reason.

For the rest of his life, Jacques wondered about the old man who had been walking down a dark road at midnight—that classic hour of mystery. He realized that the old man had walked toward him down a deserted road, from a direction where there was nothing of note except . . . the cemetery.

"I muse often," Jacques wrote at the end of his account, "about this gallant Delphin Rambert, sleeping in the cemetery of Saint-Ciers, not far from my people, who wanted so desperately one night to come and talk to me about them, and who sometimes, even now perhaps, shuffles past my uncle's house toward the town in the misty night. . . ."

As Patrick McCurdy came to the end of this eerie tale, he felt strangely close to his uncle. Jacques had died peacefully in his sleep, at the age of eighty, in 1978. Patrick feels that no doubt Jacques finally has the answer to his haunting puzzle.

# Tulsa's Trick
# or Treat

According to ancient tradition, Halloween (also called All-Hallow's Eve and Samhain) is the time when the walls between worlds have grown thin and spirits may walk the earth from sunset to sunrise. So it is no surprise that people who are home that night open their doors to find a front porch full of ghosts, goblins, and monsters calling out "Trick or treat!"

On one Halloween in Tulsa, Oklahoma, however, it was the trick-or-treaters who got the surprise.

A group of children knocked on the front door of a duplex home on the south side of Tulsa. It was answered by a distinguished-looking silver-haired man in black tie and tails. Decorating these formal garments were the official ribbons, badges, and medals of a European prince.

"Good evening, little monsters," he said, and then laughed villainously.

"It's Dracula!" one awed trick-or-treater called out.

"You are so right."

Little did any of these apprentice ghosts and goblins know

that the man in the tuxedo was telling the truth. His name is William Dagget-Eletsky. By birth, rank, and bloodline he is also Vladimar II, Prince of Elets. He is the great-nephew (fifteen generations removed) of Prince Vlad Teppes of Wallachia, the historical figure who was the model for Dracula, the lord of the vampires.

"His name was Vlad Tepes the third, Volvode [Prince] of Wallachia, which is now a part of Romania. In spite of popular belief, he did not live in Transylvania, which is next to Wallachia, although he did visit there on occasion," Dagget-Eletsky later told reporter Brad Sinor of the *Jenks Journal*.

The name Dracula became synonymous with vampires after the publication of the novel of the same name by Bram Stoker in 1897. What few people outside of Europe knew was that when the character of Dracula spoke of a "human" life lived in the Balkans centuries before, he was telling the truth.

"The name Dracula actually developed because of his father, Vlad II," Dagget-Eletsky said. "Vlad II was given the leadership of the Order of the Dragon and as such became known as Dracul, which translates as variously as the Dragon, the Demon or the Devil. His son, Vlad III, was known as Dracula, the son of the Demon. Vlad III made every effort to live up to the family tradition."

Vlad is remembered as being both a hero and a vicious tyrant, depending on who you talk to. His countrymen celebrate the statesman-warrior who defended his homeland against the invading Turkish armies. Yet the fact that he reputedly ordered the deaths of more than 150,000 people, as many political enemies as foreigners, is not forgotten. His favorite method of execution—slow death by impalement—earned him the nickname "Vlad the Impaler."

Dagget-Eletsky's family has kept detailed records and documentation of their bloodlines and ancestries. Their family tree is detailed in the small print of a chart that is over seven and a half feet long. They number among their ancestors much of the royalty of Europe.

"Our connection to Vlad comes from when his half-sister, Hannah, married my ancestor," said Dagget-Eletsky.

Vlad Tepes is not the only notable name in the Dagget-Eletsky family tree. In a line that they can trace as far back as the sixteenth century B.C. can be found distant "cousins" such as Genghis Khan and Catherine the Great, czarina of all the Russias.

"I guess I do have quite a family tree," Dagget-Eletsky understated.

When reporter Brad Sinor asked his age, Dagget-Eletsky smiled warily. Half jokingly, or so Sinor thought, Dagget-Eletsky said he was born in the 1480s. When pressed, he admitted to actually being only seventy years old.

Though born and raised in America, he spent a good portion of his life traveling the world as a sailor with the merchant marines. It was during these travels that he first came to Tulsa. So when he retired from the merchant marines as a captain a few years ago, he relocated to Oklahoma.

"The people in this part of the country are probably some of the friendliest that I have ever encountered," he said.

The two men shook hands after the interview and Sinor left, going home to write his story.

Back at the newspaper offices, Brad Sinor studied a copy of the *Jenks Journal* that had just rolled off the press. It would be another couple of hours before the weekly paper would be picked up, distributed to racks all over the tiny bedroom community, and mailed out to subscribers.

He was pleased that the editor had been able to find room in the latest issue to run his picture of Dagget-Eletsky along with the story. Of the two photos that he had taken earlier, amid jokes by the older man that he might not show up on film, this was definitely the more sinister one—and apropos, considering his family tree. One of the other reporters had suggested that the second photo made the prince look more like the actor Alan Hale, Jr., the skipper on *Gilligan's Island*, than royalty.

Sinor had been impressed with the man. "I do take my family seriously, but I am not above having a bit of fun with it, either," Dagget-Eletsky had told him.

On the spur of the moment, Sinor decided to phone the prince and let him know that the story had been used in this week's issue. He was quite disturbed to discover that the notebook which contained all his notes from the interview, along with the prince's address and phone number, was nowhere to be found.

Annoyed, Sinor picked up the heavy yellow Tulsa phone book. However, there was no listing for the name, despite the fact that he had looked it up less than ten days before, when he had made an appointment for the interview.

"I'm sorry, sir, but there is nothing listed under any combination of that name," a phone operator told him. That news gave Sinor a very odd feeling.

"This is getting a little bit strange," he told one of the other reporters.

"Maybe it was one of the older phone books," the man suggested.

That was a very distinct possibility. Scattered over the newsroom were local phone books for Tulsa and the suburban communities. Sinor went through all of them but could find nothing.

"This is getting weirder by the minute. But considering who this guy is, I'm not surprised," he said to the newspaper's photographer, who had stopped in to invite him to lunch.

Later that evening Sinor drove to the south side of Tulsa, carefully following the exact route he had taken to the prince's home the first time. The duplex was there, just as he remembered it. But this time there were no lights, the window shades were pulled tightly closed, and no one answered his knock.

"You looking for somebody?" The voice belonged to a man trimming a hedge next door.

"Yes, the man who lived here. Has he moved?"

"Lived there? I really don't think that anyone has been living there for quite a while," the neighbor said.

Sinor stood there, nonplussed. Right at that moment, he was certain he heard a strange flapping sound. Like the wings of a bird—or a bat—flying away.

To this day, he has never located William Dagget-Eletsky, who could be anywhere. So if you have a distinguished-looking older man for a neighbor, with a penchant for tuxedos—and perhaps night flying—be sure to let us know.

# Subterranean Spirits

There's something different about the big old house on Eighth Street in Pueblo, Colorado. Built in 1929 for a prominent businessman, the beige adobe structure with the protruding second-floor balcony blends in with the other houses in the old, established neighborhood . . . except for the ghosts.

Gloria Alzado (all the names in this story have been changed with the exception of the ghosts) knew there was something strange about the house right away. It made her feel uncomfortable. But she couldn't pinpoint the problem. Besides, the house was in a good neighborhood, and the price was within her budget.

After a while, Gloria noticed that the lights in the basement seemed to have a life of their own. They went on and off at random. And there was the furniture that moved of its own accord. It was as if someone unseen were living downstairs—someone who watched her every time she went into the basement. One day, after Gloria had settled in, her friend Marsha came to visit and brought her eight-year-old son, Danny

115

along. Marsha was curious to see what Gloria had done with the house, since she knew the previous owner, Barbara Woods. While Gloria and Marsha chatted in the kitchen, Danny watched television in the living room.

Suddenly Danny burst into the kitchen and announced, "The lady I told you about is standing on the stairs. She smiled at me this time."

Marsha explained that whenever they drove past the house in previous visits, when Barbara Woods lived there, Danny claimed he had seen a young woman standing on the balcony. On their last visit, Danny had seen the young woman in the window of the front bedroom. To top that off, he also said he saw her standing in Barbara Woods's sewing room.

According to Danny, Marsha continued, the young woman had auburn hair and always wore a pink and white dress. Neither woman had any idea what Danny was talking about.

Just a few nights later, Gloria was unable to sleep. She sat up in bed watching television when a movement caught her eye. She turned slowly and saw a young woman—who completely matched the description Danny had given—carefully picking up the knickknacks and toiletries on Gloria's dresser.

Gloria watched the woman for a few moments, wondering who she was and why she was in Gloria's bedroom. She couldn't possibly be a ghost—she looked too real!

"What are you doing here?" Gloria finally asked.

The woman turned around, surprised. She carefully looked at Gloria and then smiled. Then she disappeared.

The next day, Gloria phoned Marsha for advice. Barbara Woods's house obviously was haunted and Gloria was uncertain what to do about it. Marsha even phoned Barbara for more information. Eventually all three women agreed Gloria should call in a psychic. Barbara suggested inviting a local man by the name of Brad Simonson to "cleanse the house of psychic energies."

In fact, Barbara told Gloria that the house had a history of strange occurrences. Barbara was a teacher and one of her classes was on the science of the mind. One night a visiting student had the most unusual experience in the house. The student said she felt she had lived in the house before as another person—a woman who committed suicide upstairs. The student said she could see herself "lying in state" on the porch outside the living room.

Brad Simonson agreed to investigate Gloria's house. He claimed to have the ability not only to see spirits but to communicate with them.

When he entered the house he immediately announced he could feel a lot of psychic energy. He slowly climbed the steps of the front staircase to the second floor, then stopped on the forth and fifth steps. "I can feel a woman, about twenty-six years old, wearing a pink satin dress, standing here," said Brad. "She's standing here and clutching the banister, just as I am. She can see someone she loves in the dining room offering some type of affection to another woman. I can feel anger and jealousy."

Brad explained that inanimate objects like the staircase can absorb psychic energies and record them like a cassette player. A sensitive can feel the energy, which can evoke the image and the emotion.

Upstairs, Brad stopped at the master bathroom and held on to the sink. "Someone was close to death in this room. I can feel an older man having a heart attack and holding on to the sink." He paused for a moment and moved to the side of the tub.

"I think a young girl committed suicide here. But her spirit is not in the house. Nor is the man's. There's someone else here."

Brad continued walking through the rest of the house. They had not yet gone into the basement but had now returned to the kitchen, where the basement door was located. As Brad's foot touched the top step of the basement stairs, he looked surprised.

"Wait here," he instructed, turning on the basement light. He left Gloria alone for about ten minutes before he returned. Brad had gone off to meditate and, as it turned out, communicate with what he was surprised to discover.

"There are two spirits still in the house," he explained. "But not the ghosts I've described so far—these are two new ones! A husband and wife. The young man said his name is Craig McDermitt or McEntire, or some name like that. His wife's name is Julie."

Brad continued his amazing story: "They originally came from California in 1942, when he was drafted to fight in World War II. Craig was stationed here at the air base near Pueblo and they rented these basement rooms. Not long after, Craig was killed in a training accident, and his spirit returned to the house. He feels responsible for the accident and is afraid to move on to the next world.

"Craig is a young man in his early twenties, blond and very good-looking. Julie is about seventeen, tall and slender with auburn hair parted in the middle. She was pregnant when Craig was killed, and died in childbirth soon after. They are both buried here in Pueblo. She says that she still loves Craig and does not want to leave him here alone."

Brad went on to explain that Craig was very angry about his death. He was afraid that he and Julie would be separated if they moved on. So Craig planned to stay in the house forever, since this was the only place that he'd ever been happy. However, if Gloria still wanted her house cleansed of ghosts, Brad was willing to perform an exorcism.

Gloria thought carefully about all she'd heard. She considered herself a very conservative person and never spent too much time thinking about ghosts or the spirit world. But the presence of two spirits in the house did not frighten her. And since she'd seen Julie, she felt more at ease in the house, even in the basement.

"I believe that I saw Julie for a reason," Gloria said. "I think she trusts me, and I am willing to help them until they are ready to move on. As long as they are comfortable here, I am comfortable to have them stay."

The story of the subterranean spirits on Eighth Street was written up by reporter Nancy A. Cucci for a local newspaper. Not long after Nancy's article appeared, a local farmer found the remains of an old World War II Army training plane while plowing an unused portion of his field. Apparently the plane crashed there and was not recovered. Nancy Cucci checked the Army records and confirmed that several men, including the navigator, were killed in an accident. The navigator's name was Craig McDermitt.

# The Last Guest of the Home Comfort Hotel

Ghost towns in Colorado are disappearing at a steady pace, destroyed by fire, the elements, and trespassers, or razed by developers. So far, St. Elmo is an exception. The town is nestled into an ancient flood plain surrounding Chalk Creek; the surrounding forest and breathtaking mountain scenery draw large numbers of tourists in good weather. It's been called the most haunting and the best preserved of Colorado's ghost towns, and no one knows how right they are. . . .

The town owes its continued existence to one family, the Starks, who were the sole continuous residents through much of the twentieth century. According to eyewitnesses, at least one of them, Annabelle Stark Ward, still watches over the town twenty-five years after her death. And she watches over it from her vantage point in the Home Comfort Hotel on Poplar Street.

Poplar is the main business street and the Home Comfort sits halfway down the street, across from the town hall. The hotel is one of the few two-story buildings left; it has a weathered wooden false front, incongruous extensions and outbuildings, and stands out from the twenty-odd tin-roofed log buildings that remain standing.

Prospectors came into the Chalk Creek area in the 1870s and the town of St. Elmo was born. It was originally called Forest City, but the name had to be changed because the post office wouldn't accept it; there already was a Forest City in California. So in 1880 the city officially became known as St. Elmo. Why that name was picked isn't precisely known. It may have been a popular novel of the day; it may be because of the phenomena of St. Elmo's fire in the region.

In 1881, St. Elmo became a stopping point for the Denver, South Park, and Pacific Railroad. Almost immediately a cycle of bust and boom began, since the town's fortunes were based on mining. It was about then that Anton Stark came to town. He'd brought cattle to sell and was so impressed with the possibilities that he sent for his wife and put down roots. Stark became a section boss in the mines and his wife Anna ran both the hotel and general store. The Starks' general store also became the post office and telegraph office.

Anna Stark was by all accounts a tough, humorless woman who controlled her three children with an iron hand. She believed that Tony, Roy, and Annabelle were too good to associate with the other townsfolk and discouraged them from doing anything except work. So her hotel was the cleanest in town and her meals were the best. As long as the mines were open, the Starks did fairly well.

Annabelle, the only daughter, grew up in the town of rough miners and hard women. She was a very attractive girl with a pleasing personality. But her mother curbed her activities and associations even more sternly than her brothers' were. In her entire life, Annabelle was allowed to attend only one dance.

Anna always thought St. Elmo would be a valuable area

and that mining would pick up again. As people moved out of town, Anna bought up property at tax sales. But in the 1920s, when St. Elmo lost its railroad line, the town was mostly deserted. Roy and Tony spent years trying to interest developers into reopening the mines, but they were never successful. It was Roy who saw the possibilities of tourism. He got the family in the business of leasing cabins to tourists.

After Anton Stark's death, the family couldn't earn a living with their cabin rentals and tourist trade at the store. Reluctantly, Anna sent Annabelle to work at the telegraph office in Salida, a much larger town about twenty miles away. In Salida, however, Annabelle met and married a Mr. Ward in 1921 or 1922. She sent her family a telegram to announce her marriage—and to inform them she was moving to Trinidad! Annabelle had finally made her escape.

But neither the marriage nor the escape worked very well. There is much speculation over what happened during the next several years, but the result is that Annabelle was eventually forced to return home, where she remained for the rest of her life.

In 1943 Roy died; Anna Stark died a short time later. Tony and Annabelle continued to live alone in the ghost town. Because they were finally freed of their mother's demanding cleanliness, or perhaps because of the harsh environment, the two siblings abandoned all niceties. There had never been indoor plumbing at the hotel. There was no longer electricity. The two rarely bathed or changed clothes. They threw nothing away and slowly filled all the rooms of the hotel with trash. To the residents of the area, Annabelle became known as Dirty Annie. She appeared in a Salida grocery store wearing a dirty Army overcoat over several old sweaters and slacks. A man's hat was tied to her head with a woolen scarf. Underneath the hat was a woolen stocking cap through which hair had grown through holes in the cap.

Annabelle could be nice enough to people who came to purchase soda or candy in the Home Comfort Hotel's lobby/store. But she also was fond of wandering around town with a rifle to protect her property. She had a propensity for feeding chipmunks, and dozens of them would greet her on her rounds.

Finally both Tony and Annabelle were sent to a mental institution, but a friend secured their release. Tony died soon after that and Annabelle lingered in a Salida nursing home until her death in 1960. They left their property to the friend.

Not long after Annabelle's death, the friend's grandchildren were playing in a lower room of the hotel. All of a sudden the doors of the room closed by themselves and the temperature dropped about twenty degrees. The children clung together in terror until the temperature began rising and the doors opened. They would not play in the building again.

One of the older grandchildren, in her twenties, undertook to clean the hotel. She and some friends washed the walls, scrubbed the floors, and made minor repairs. Many times they would put away all of the buckets and brushes, only to find them in the middle of the floor the next day. When it first happened, it was thought they'd forgotten to put everything away. So the granddaughter and friends made doubly sure by putting the buckets and brushes in a closet and padlocking the doors. When they returned, they again found a bucket and brush in the middle of the room they'd been cleaning. They finally—and fearfully—decided someone was helping them—probably Anna Stark, who might have thought they weren't being clean enough.

Several years ago a skier, whose family had a summer cabin in St. Elmo, actually saw the hotel's ghost. She was skiing down Poplar Street at dusk. Her eyes were drawn to the second story of the hotel. In one of the windows stood a shapely young woman dressed in white. The woman was holding back the curtains and looking out the window. At first the skier thought it was some trick of light. She knew that the owner, who had the only keys to the hotel, was out of the country. As she watched the figure on the second floor, she saw it move. She realized the figure was watching a group of snowmobilers riding up and down the street. And the woman had a disapproving look on her face.

The skier flagged down the snowmobilers and asked them to leave, since snowmobiling was illegal in St. Elmo. When they had gone, she turned back to the hotel. The woman was still watching. She nodded at the skier and then disappeared.

The next day the skier went back to the hotel and found that all the windows and doors were secured. When the owner returned, the two women searched the hotel but found nothing had been disturbed. After some discussion, they decided it was Annabelle's ghost—perhaps now young, pretty, and reliving a better time—still watching over the town.

In fact, for the other part-time residents of St. Elmo, and down in the valley in the rest of Chaffee County, the talk sometimes turns to Annabelle. They wonder just how far Annabelle will go to protect what belongs to her. Those who knew her in her later days, when she wandered the street with her shotgun, don't want to find out.

St. Elmo can be reached by Route 162, a two-lane dirt road off of Highway 285.

# The Tower of London

T he Tower of London is one of the most widely visited tourist attractions in all of Britain. It has a long history dating back to William the Conqueror. The Tower is actually a collection of buildings, including, among others, the White, Bell, Beauchamp, and Bloody towers; in its day it has served as royal residence, prison, treasury, and even menagerie. Norman/Gothic in style, it is primarily built of good gray British stone, although some of the component structures are of brick.

Its most infamous entry is the Traitors' Gate, a water gate accessible from the River Thames. For centuries, barges stopped at its dreaded steps, disgorging prisoners of greater or lesser degrees of fame, all of whom had had the misfortune of offending their reigning sovereign.

Sir Thomas More, later to be named a saint, lost his life within the tower's confines, as did Edward V, who was murdered, some say, by his uncle Richard III. Lady Jane Grey, queen of England for only nine days, was executed there, as was Catherine Howard, the fifth wife of Henry VIII. There are tales attesting to the spectral appearances of them all.

Elizabeth Tudor, later to rule England for forty-five years, was imprisoned within its walls by command of her own sister, known as Bloody Mary. Elizabeth was one of the fortunate few who left the tower with her neck intact; her mother was not so blessed. Anne Boleyn, Henry's second wife, fell before the headsman's sword. They say her ghost walks the tower precincts. There's even a song, more than four centuries old, about her wanderings:

> With 'er 'ead tooked underneath 'er arm
> She walks the Bloody Tower.
> With 'er 'ead tooked underneath 'er arm
> She prowls the midnight hour.

Even during her lifetime, some claimed that Queen Anne had supernatural powers. One of the charges against her was that she had used witchcraft against the king. To this day there are those who purport that Anne Boleyn's ghost need not wait for midnight to be seen, that her spirit is restless still, that she has the power to make her presence known to those with the eyes to see, the ears to hear. One such individual, herself a psychic, claims to have shared Anne Boleyn's last moments in a unique way.

On a rare sunlit day in late August, Roberta Klein-Mendelson and her husband, Fred, visited the Tower of London. The day began on an unusual note. Fred, never one to yield to the blandishments of sidewalk peddlers, stopped at a stall outside the tower walls to purchase a bunch of flowers for his wife. She tucked them into the enormous canvas bag she had toted all over Europe that summer.

Roberta remembers very little of the actual tour of the building, except that there were many flights of stairs to be climbed, and that the sight of the crown jewels alone was worth the price of admission.

The tour terminated at the edge of the tower green, which was well populated by other tourists, the famous tower ravens, and the equally famous Beefeater Guards, gorgeous in brilliant scarlet uniforms designed in the sixteenth century. On the green was a conspicuous black sign indicating the site of the original scaffold. Its location did not seem correct to Roberta.

She approached the nearest Beefeater, a man towering several inches above six feet, with iron-gray hair and inviting smile. "Is this really the site of the original scaffold? I believed it was located over there." Roberta pointed.

"Yes, you're quite right, miss. It was just there, but we've recently reseeded the green, so the placard was moved. Been here before, have you?"

Roberta hadn't, but she didn't bother to answer. Her feet began to move of their own accord in the indicated direction. Suddenly the crowds of tourists, the Beefeaters, and even her husband, were gone.

At her feet, small yellow flowers bloomed in the interstices between the cobblestones. She stood in an open doorway. Behind her were sobbing women standing in front of a large hearth, a bright fire in its grate. On a table was the half-drained glass of wine she had just drunk. She could still taste its dregs in her mouth. She said, "I am ready, my lords."

As she moved through the portal, the rich black silk of her skirt rustled. Glancing down, she could see a thread of crimson petticoat and black velvet slippers peeking from under its hem.

Roberta, more fascinated than fearful, was able to feel the terror of the spirit that possessed her and realized the tremendous effort required to maintain the calm facade.

The walk to the scaffold was short, but interminable. An

errant breeze ruffled her black lace veil, and the entity called Anne stifled a scream.

She moved through the ranks of those assembled to watch royalty die, toward the steep stairs of the scaffold. At its foot, the halberdiers who escorted her took her arms gently, as befitted one who has been crowned and anointed. They cut off the possibility of flight, had there been a way out.

With them at her sides, she ascended the stairs. Before her, a priest droned his interminable prayers. She was permitted to speak her piece, but concern for her daughter bound her tongue.

They stripped her of cloak and gown and veil, as was the custom. In her petticoat she faced those witnesses. Mercifully, a blindfold was tied about her eyes, shutting out the curious stares. She was helped to kneel. Her head was guided to the block, her arms and shoulders carefully adjusted to clear the blade's path. The bared nape of her neck felt the tickle of breeze created by the sword's upswing.

Then there was only darkness.

A moment later she felt moisture, thought perhaps it was her own blood. She quickly realized, however, that it was merely water. Someone was trying to help her to drink. There were anxious murmurs around her. Roberta, again the sole inhabitant of her body, opened her eyes.

"Are you all right, miss?" A small crowd of concerned onlookers had gathered.

Roberta was momentarily disoriented until she caught sight of her Fred's face and remembered who and where she was. "I'm fine, thanks. Just a little light-headed." She had to stifle a smile when the pun registered.

Roberta got to her feet. At her side was a shadowy form. It wended its way out through the onlookers, but apparently no one save Roberta noticed. The figure was that of a woman in a long gown, a sixteenth-century coif and veil. She beckoned to Roberta, who followed. The specter glided to a part of the curtain wall whose masonry didn't match the rest of the stone structure. The figure seemed to dissolve into the wall.

"Odd that you should wander over here, miss." The solicitous Beefeater had followed her. "There's a legend about this stretch of wall. The official history of the tower says that Queen Anne Boleyn was interred in the church of St. Peter. But there are those who claim she was really laid to rest right here in the wall. Some folk say they've seen her ghost wandering hereabouts."

Roberta asked, "You wouldn't be one of those who've seen her?"

The guard reddened. "Me, miss? Do I look like the sort who believes in spirits? But what about you? Some might say you look like you saw a ghost." Roberta swears there was a twinkle in his eye.

Roberta smiled at him. "Who knows what I've seen? I'm still a bit dizzy." Although certain that he too had seen the figure, Roberta was reluctant to discuss it. Nevertheless, she took the bunch of flowers from her tote, extricated a red carnation, and laid it at the foot of the wall.

The Beefeater nodded as if they shared a secret. "They say Queen Anne was partial to gillyflowers."

The site of the scaffold, the rumored location of Anne Boleyn's grave, the selection of her favorite flower . . . were these all coincidences, or something more? Can ghosts appear in broad daylight, visible only to select onlookers? You decide.

# The Lavender Lady of Lemp House

S adness hangs like cobwebs in the darkened hallways of the Lemp mansion in St. Louis, Missouri. There's a nasty ambience inside, as though this were the quintessential haunted house. Built in the early 1860s, it's a huge boxlike structure of whitewashed brick facing De Mencil Street on one side and the Mississippi River on the other. Nine enormous windows glower down at the streetside traffic. The local pedestrians hurry past the house in respectful silence.

They know the stories.

Beyond the heavy double doors of oak and glass are thirty-three rooms of faded Victorian elegance. The parlor stands to the right of the main entrance. Inside are a gorgeous hand-painted ceiling and several carved mantels of African mahogany. On the west wall hangs an oil painting of Lillian Lemp, known in her day as the Lavender Lady, the stunning spouse of William Lemp, Jr.

In the atrium behind the parlor, the Lemp family raised exotic plants and birds. They are gone now, but the ceiling is still painted in broad leaves, a clever afterthought originally intended to heighten the feeling of jungle enclosure. Among the other rooms on the main floor is a cavernous kitchen and a regally outfitted bathroom. The bedrooms are on the second floor, the servants' quarters on the third. There are also a skylight and observation deck on the third floor.

No one spends much time up there anymore—no one of flesh and blood, at any rate.

Throughout its life the house has done duty as an office, a private residence, skid row housing, and, most currently, a restaurant. Patrons and workers have reported the uncomfortable sensation of being watched by something unseen. Phantom voices have been heard, usually accompanying some kind of poltergeist phenomenon like trembling furniture or flying crockery. There's an old piano in the bar that has the disturbing habit of playing by itself, usually when the lid is securely closed. Brandy glasses are said to have levitated from the table they were sitting on and shattered on the floor several feet away. The spectral image of a monkey face repeatedly shows up on snapshots when no monkey was anywhere nearby to pose for the picture.

Not surprisingly, the living Lemps were almost as spooky as the mansion they once occupied. Part of the house's fame is directly attributable to the family's prominence. At the turn of the century, the Lemp brewery was the third largest in the nation. The family was one of the wealthiest, with holdings well into the millions. But the Lemps were an unhappy bunch, with a penchant for extreme eccentricity and suicide.

John Adam Lemp introduced a lager beer to St. Louis in 1838 which almost instantly became a regional favorite. John's fortunes skyrocketed after that. When he passed away in 1862, he left behind a thriving enterprise on the brink of becoming an empire.

John Adam's son, William, took over for him. Under his

very competent administration, the Lemp brewery acquired its own transportation system and expanded to eleven city blocks. Lemp beer was sold internationally and by the 1880s had become as well known as Budweiser is today.

Paradoxically, the family troubles began around this time. The first casualty was Frederick Lemp, William's son, who had been groomed to head the dynasty. Frederick was brilliant, energetic, and exceptionally well liked. He once designed a poster featuring a woman revealing her pointed, high-button shoe that read: "Women also drink Lemp Beer." The poster was used effectively in a national advertising campaign, but it ruffled the fur of the ultraconservative town fathers. It quickly became a local scandal and Frederick was thrown out of the St. Louis Leader's Club for introducing sex into advertising.

Frederick worked himself literally to death, succumbing to heart failure at the age of twenty-eight. William could not bring himself to accept the loss of his favorite son. For three years he gradually withdrew from the world, and on a cool morning in 1904 he shot himself in his office at the family mansion.

Like a curse, Frederick's death tainted the lives of the surviving Lemps. None would ever know happiness and three would ultimately follow William's suicidal example. Sixteen years after his self-inflicted demise, William's daughter Elsa did herself in. Her marriage had been stormy and there were rumors that she had actually been murdered by her husband. But it was finally determined that depression and ill health were the real factors that led her to suicide. Like her father, Elsa shot herself with a revolver in the early morning hours.

Elsa's brother, Will, Jr., was running the business at that time. He inherited a sizable fortune, which he wasted no time in spending. He lived imperiously, surrounding himself with a whole tribe of fawning, liveried servants. Will, Jr., also built country houses and accumulated an incredible stock of Oriental draperies, carriage horses, antiques, and bric-a-brac. So enormous was his art collection that three vaults were annexed to the rear of the house to contain it.

Will Lemp, Jr., had it all, it seemed. Yet money and power did not improve his disposition. He was said to be unrelentingly hostile toward anyone he believed had crossed him, even if that person was a member of his immediate family.

In 1899 he married Lillian Handlan, the daughter of a wealthy manufacturer of railroad supplies. Lillian was nicknamed the Lavender Lady because of her habit of attiring herself—and her horse and carriage—exclusively in lavender.

Will, Jr., showed her off, along with his other ornaments. He was also fond of indulging her, but in a cynical, mean-spirited sort of way. Each morning Lillian was given a thousand-dollar bill. "Spend it all," he admonished her, "or you'll get nothing tomorrow!"

That was a tall order in the late nineteenth century, but by all reports, Lillian had no difficulty complying with it. Will, Jr., divorced her nevertheless, which gave the newspapers of the period a ton of exploitable scandal.

Lillian countersued. At the trial she revealed that one of her husband's favorite pastimes was to try to run over the people he didn't like with his horse and carriage. If this insane action failed to intimidate his enemies he would fire a couple of shots over their heads. Will, Jr., replied that Lillian sometimes smoked cigarettes in the house. This set the tide of public opinion against her, and she lost the case.

After the divorce, the Lavender Lady went into seclusion, where she slowly languished and quietly died. Will, Jr., became increasingly misanthropic. More and more he avoided human contact whenever possible.

The mansion stood only a few blocks from the brewery. Both had been built over a network of caves, which he began to use to get to and from his office. Years before, Will, Jr., had built a swimming pool, ballroom, and vaudeville stage underground. Now he could spend as much time as he wanted in this very private place.

When prohibition was enacted into law in 1919, the brewery closed. The plant, which had once been valued at $7 million, brought only $588,500 when it was sold in 1922. Will, Jr., let everything slide after that. On the morning of December 29 he was alone in his office on South Thirteenth Street. After he had dismissed his secretary and completed a brief telephone conversation with his second wife, he shot himself through the heart with a revolver.

The fourth suicide was Charles, perhaps the strangest Lemp of the lot. He had a morbid attachment to the family mansion and insisted on living in it despite its dreadful past. As he grew older, Charles became increasingly neurotic and took to wearing gloves all the time for fear of contamination. He lived to a ripe old age, but the house finally got to him. He killed himself in 1949 when he was seventy-seven years old. Just as William, Will, Jr., and Elsa had done, Charles used a pistol.

Unlike his brothers and sister, Edwin Lemp wisely chose not to live in the family mansion. He had a sprawling estate in the suburban community of Kirkwood, but was always afraid to be left alone. Edwin entertained as often as possible and had his servants stay with him around the clock. When he died of natural causes at the age of ninety, the line died with him.

All the Lemps are gone now, at least in body. But they may still be causing problems.

When the mansion was being refurbished into a restaurant, a live-in painter was hired to help with the renovations. He was berthed in the Lavender Lady's old bedroom on the second floor. Every morning he complained that his sleep had been disturbed by the sound of horses coming out of the carriage house and walking around the cobblestone courtyard underneath his window.

But there were no cobblestones anywhere near the empty carriage house—only a grass yard. The mystery remained unresolved until later that summer. As the heat grew more intense, the grass began to dry up in little squares. When the yard was dug up, a tile courtyard was discovered about six inches beneath the topsoil. All of the tiles dated from 1878 and were so attractive that they were used to cover the basement floor.

Animals do not voluntarily enter the Lemp house. There may be an excellent reason for this. Once the restoration was in full swing, the new owner hired his son to act as night watchman. He had a friendly Doberman pinscher named Shadow who would never leave his side. When the watchman arrived for work one day, Shadow would not follow him into the house. Instead she cowered, whined, and even tried to bite him. Eventually the dog was tied up behind the back entrance, and about a half hour later she mysteriously disappeared.

About three years after the restaurant opened, an elderly woman came in for lunch. The owner's son was working in the dining room at this time and the woman called him over to her table. She told him that she had been one of the servants who had discovered the body of Charles Lemp after he had committed suicide. Lemp had not gone to the great beyond alone, she said. He had taken his dog with him, shooting the animal in the heart before he had put the gun barrel to his head.

The dog had been a Doberman pinscher.

Psychics from as far away as Los Angeles and New York

have explored the Lemp mansion. Many have come away convinced the place is haunted. The consensus among them is that Charles is responsible for most of the paranormal activity. Many have confirmed, without being familiar with the family history, that he shot himself.

If Charles does haunt Lemp house, he seems to be interested in drawing attention to himself. On one occasion, a reporter from the *St. Louis Post Dispatch* and a famous psychic toured the mansion from top to bottom. As they got ready to leave, every table in the empty dining room began to shake uncontrollably, sending plates, silverware, and condiments crashing to the floor.

Another time a voice was heard to say "Hi, Mom; Hi, Mom" as the restaurant owner's wife entered a room. The woman didn't recognize the voice, which, quite understandably, scared the daylights out of her.

Aside from Charles, there seems to be a second troubled personality skulking about the grounds. When the house was first being refurbished, two ladies dropped in one day and asked where the Lemps had kept the monkey boy. They said that as children they had often seen a face in an upper-story window that fit that description and wondered what had become of this unfortunate person.

Subsequent investigation revealed that the birth records did not agree on the number of Lemp children. There was even an old rumor that a deformed child was once kept locked away in the attic. The rumor has since been chillingly confirmed by the fact that a monkey face continually appears on photographs taken inside the house.

The Lemp mansion is located at 3322 De Mencil Street in south St. Louis. It's a restaurant now and serves lunch and dinner. The restaurant is closed on Monday and on Saturday afternoons.

Whatever stalks there seems intent on remaining. Though

Charles, the monkey boy, and the others usually restrict their activities to the wee hours or to times when trade is relatively slow, psychic phenomena are extremely unpredictable. Who knows when the spirits may get lively again? Maybe today, tomorrow, or the next time you drop in for lunch.

# The Invisible Roommate

Judith Tanaka, her husband Kenji, and their young so
David were dyed-in-the-wool Wisconsinites. But in 197
when Kenji accepted an executive position with an interna
tional company, the Tanaka family gave up sledding, parkas
and boots for several years in sunny Japan.

The Tanakas (not their real names) lived in the Aoyama—
pronounced *Ow-yama*—district, a residential section o
downtown Tokyo. It was a typical apartment for that area
long and narrow, sparsely furnished. It was also a mirro
image of the adjacent apartment, connected to the Tanak
apartment by a common wall. The two apartments forme
one small dwelling, similar to an American row house o
town house.

Traditionally in Japan, the living room is also the bedroom
Each night Judy and her husband slept on a mat called
futon. In the morning the futon was rolled up and the bedroom
again became the living room.

The living room was located at the front of the apartmen

David's bedroom was in the rear. Between them was a kitchen, and just off the back was a bathroom.

There was nothing unusual about the Tanaka apartment and the family lived there peacefully until the summer of 1973, when David celebrated his twelfth birthday. That's when the strange things started happening. . . .

Judy was in the bathroom one day when suddenly the light switch—located on a wall outside the bathroom—flipped off. The room, naturally, went dark. Thinking it was her husband or son playing a joke, she yelled, "Cut it out, you guys!"

But then Judy remembered she was home alone.

Lights in other rooms turned themselves on and off. The radio and the record player suddenly became difficult to operate, as though they played only when they felt like it.

There was also the puzzle of the disappearing geta. Japanese tradition calls for the removal of shoes when entering the home, and the shoes are left by the front door. Because the bathroom tiles are cold, a pair of sandals, or getas, are always kept by the bathroom door. When someone goes to the bathroom, he or she slips on the getas, slipping them off again on the way out of the room so that they are in the proper position for the next person to put on. It usually becomes an automatic motion.

One day Judy noticed that one of the getas was missing from the bathroom. It was possible someone might have forgotten to slip off the getas and walked away in them, but then both sandals would be missing. Only one missing sandal made no sense.

Judy ransacked the apartment but could not find the missing geta. In fact, she searched for three weeks before giving up.

Meanwhile, David, typical of many young people, was not keeping his room tidy. He didn't even roll up his futon.

Finally, after much nagging, David rolled up the futon—tha was the day they finally found the geta. It was under David' futon.

It didn't seem possible that David would have slept on wooden sandal for three weeks and not notice. "I can't imag ine why he didn't feel it under his body," said Judy. "It' like the reverse of *The Princess and the Pea*."

Not long after the missing sandal was found, Judy wa casually talking to her next-door neighbor Edward Kelly (no his real name). By chance, Kelly told her about the strang things happening in *his* apartment.

Edward Kelly, a Canadian gentleman, lived in the mirro image apartment next door. His bedroom was located on th other side of David's bedroom wall. It, too, was sparsel furnished.

In Kelly's bedroom, to diffuse the glare of the bare lig bulb, he had bought a large white paper globe (often calle a Japanese lantern). After covering the light bulb with th lantern, he had hung a cord through the hole in the bottom the lantern. And to that cord he had attached a pair of mini ture getas as a decoration.

Kelly had come home late one night and was groping the darkness of his bedroom. He was trying to find the lante cord so he could turn on the light. But it was nowhere to I found. He gave up trying to find it, got undressed in the dar and went to sleep.

In the morning he discovered the cord—getas and all— was stuffed into the hole of the paper globe. He certainl hadn't done it, and no one else had been in his apartmen No one human, that is.

Eventually Kelly decided he had an unseen roommate. On day he was listening to music in his bedroom and the stere started behaving strangely. The music would get soft, the loud, then soft, then loud, almost as though the machine were turning the volume knob by itself. Or perhaps some unseen force was moving between him and the stereo, blocking out the sound—or adjusting it.

At first Kelly thought the electrical company was adjusting power voltage. But nothing else in the room seemed affected. The overhead lantern light never changed. The other electrical appliances in the rest of the house operated normally. He had the stereo checked, but nothing was wrong.

Listening to Kelly's tales, Judy fell silent and then admitted that her family had experienced some mighty strange things themselves. In fact, the occurrences in both houses were quite similar: unexplained electrical problems, especially with music and stereo players; getas moved and illogically placed.

In trying to find out if their house was haunted, Judy came across another explanation, one which was even harder to believe or explain. There is no word in Japanese for *poltergeist*. The Japanese may not even have that concept. *Poltergeist* is a German word for "noisy ghost." Though a poltergeist may not necessarily be noisy, it is certainly a prankster. It is also not a ghost at all. Experts believe a poltergeist is a form of energy—usually created by pubescent girls and boys. Judy's son David was twelve and both she and Kelly realized that the bizarre occurrences did not start until David's twelfth birthday.

In fact, the thread that ran through all the occurrences seemed to be her son's presence. It was a very rebellious time for David, and he spent a lot of hours alone in his room— the room that was right next to Edward Kelly's bedroom.

And Judy felt she had proof that David was responsible for the poltergeist: In 1974, after a year of peculiar happenings, David visited his grandmother in Florida. While he was gone, the Japanese apartment was quiet. She and Kelly had no more odd occurrences to chat about.

David is grown up now and in the armed services. Presumably the poltergeist has not enlisted with him and might still linger in Tokyo.

# The Case of
# the Jealous Ghost

In a small New Hampshire village called Gilford, located near Lake Winnipesaukee, is a seven-room Cape Cod house built in 1765. The land was originally part of a king's grant that consisted of three thousand acres, and was passed down through generations. The land has been sold off and all that remains is three-quarters of an acre on which the house and a separate standing barn are located. The foundation of the barn is made up of tombstones, and the house is located in an area between two mountains where, according to local legends, sacrificial rites were performed.

In 1968, when the Herbert family consisted of an eighteen-month-old baby with a second child on the way, Wayne and his wife Grace decided to look for a house. Since Wayne traveled about the countryside while working as a plumber, he noticed the old house in Gilford had a FOR SALE sign on it. Call it destiny or what you will, but one day Wayne's boss sent him to this house to do some work.

Since the house was vacant, his boss gave Wayne a set of keys to gain access. He let himself into the basement so he

143

could look at what needed to be done. While working on the cellar pipes, he heard footsteps walking about on the first floor. Thinking the owner had returned, Wayne went upstairs. But no one answered his call. Perhaps the owner had gone into one of the rooms. Wayne started to search, and as soon as he set foot in the kitchen he was enveloped by a strange but warm feeling. In fact, it was a feeling that he had lived in this house before and that it always would be his house!

He never did see or find the owner. When Wayne finished work, he returned to the office and phoned his wife Grace; he suggested that she call the real estate agent who had the house listed and arrange to see it that afternoon.

When Wayne got home that night, he asked Grace how she felt about the house. To his surprise, she had the exact same feelings about the house as he did. At this point Wayne called the real estate agent and made an offer on the house, but it was rejected as too low. Wayne found out that three other couples had also tried to buy the house and their offers were higher than his. They too were turned down. Yet several days later the real estate agent called the Herberts and said the owner had decided to sell the house to them!

The reason became apparent when the Herberts sat down with the owner, a woman who had lived alone in the house, to discuss the transfer of the property. She informed them that she considered the house to be very unfriendly. She said strange things were happening . . . like the time she filled the 275-gallon oil tank, only to find it totally empty the very next day! Something kept polluting the well, and she couldn't use the water. Light bulbs kept blowing out; windows were always broken. Though she'd lived in the house for less than three years, she felt she had to get out.

Shortly after the Herberts moved in one cold January, strange things started to happen to them too. They would go out, leaving the windows open. If it rained while they were out, they would return to find the windows closed. The Herberts thought the ghost was pretty nifty . . . until a year after moving in.

It was January, about two in the morning. The new baby was a few months old, and Grace had gotten up to change his diaper. So she picked him up out of his crib and started going down the stairs. Grace had just taken a few steps when she felt two hands on her back, pushing her. She stumbled and quickly grabbed the railing. Slowly and carefully she walked down the remainder of the stairway and stood at the bottom, shaking. Though she could see no one, she felt a presence.

Aloud, and to the empty air, she said, "You know, I don't see why you're upset. I think you're just jealous because I have a baby and maybe you wanted one and couldn't have one. But if I ever feel threatened like this again, we will leave. We will be gone forever!"

The ghost apparently believed Grace, because from that point on, nothing violent happened. But other odd things occurred.

One night, after putting the children to bed, Grace was downstairs watching television, while her husband was upstairs putting a jigsaw puzzle together. All of a sudden she heard a very loud crash—like a bureau being tipped over—from upstairs. Wayne heard the same crash and thought it came from below. So when they each went to investigate, they met on the staircase. Together they went through the entire house and found nothing disturbed. Their two children were both still fast asleep.

On several occasions, the apparition of an older woman wearing a lacy Victorian dress has been seen on the second floor of the house. While the floor-length dress with its frilly collar is very clear, the woman's face is not, although one can discern that her eyes are closed. Once she was seen standing in the hallway, and another time she was seen lying on a bed in one of the second-floor bedrooms. Each time she had her arms folded or crossed across her bosom, as if she were lying in a casket!

No doubt this is the same ghost that visited Grace's brother one night. He was staying overnight in their guest room. During the night he was awakened by a female voice calling out his name. Sleepily thinking his sister had entered the room, he sat up and asked, "What do you want, sis?" But no one answered. There didn't seem to be anyone in the room. So he lay down, only to hear the same female voice call out his name twice more. By now the young man was petrified. He grabbed the blankets and spent the rest of the night on the living room couch.

Since the Herberts had told their friends many fascinating stories about the house, one night some friends suggested they try a séance. None of the participants actually knew how to perform one, but recalling what they had seen in the movies and on television, they turned off the lights, placed a lit candle in the middle of the kitchen table, and sat around it while holding hands. Then each would take a turn asking a question, hoping to get some sort of response or sign from the presence that they all felt was in the house.

Unfortunately, no one was successful. It was only after they left, and for several days, that the presence made itself known. Perhaps it had been disturbed; it became more active by making noises in every part of the house!

Rumors about the Herberts' house spread. One day they received a phone call from a psychic who lived in the area. She asked permission to visit, which they willingly gave. Once the psychic stepped through the door, she told the Herberts that everything was suddenly deathly quiet—as though she had stepped into a time warp. After walking around the house, the woman said she indeed felt a presence. And while the presence wasn't menacing, the psychic was a little frightened because she couldn't pinpoint where it was or even what it was.

When they went outside, the stillness followed them. There were no cars, no birds chirped, the leaves stopped rustling. The psychic quickly drove off, never to return.

Wayne and Grace attended a lecture given by Norm Gauthier, a psychic researcher based in New Hampshire who also taught parapsychology in evening classes at a number of colleges throughout the state. Gauthier had visited and researched haunted houses all over the United States. After the lecture the Herberts approached Gauthier, told him a little about their home, and invited him to visit them. Gauthier did visit them in February 1983, and he tape-recorded their story. Later he contacted the local historical society for additional information and also tried to find previous owners of the house.

Gauthier felt that another attempt should be made to identify the presence in the house. He discussed the case with Herb Dewey, an old friend who is an internationally known psychic and an authority on hypnosis. The two men decided to work together, and another visit to the Herberts' house was arranged, this time with the intention of placing Grace in a hypnotic trance to see if that way she might recall more details about her encounters. The Herberts greeted them and then all four went to the downstairs den. Wayne sat in one chair, Gauthier in another, and Grace and Dewey sat on the couch. The lights were dimmed and Dewey talked to Grace in a relaxed, quiet tone. In a very short time Grace was in a hypnotic trance. To get Grace in the right frame of mind, Dewey instructed her, "You will have total recall throughout this session. The purpose of this session is to gain information about the spirit that is in the house. Concentrate on drifting through the house, not just this room but throughout the building.

"In your mind, visualize the spirit that may be in this house and concentrate on what she looks like, what her face is like, the shape of the body, what her name is. I want you to sense the mood of the spirit as well as the spirit's age. Somewhere in the house is a calendar; I would like you to record the time that the spirit passed on to the other side. You will see the date in your mind."

Grace seemed ready to answer questions, so Gauthier handed Dewey a list they'd prepared. The questions were read aloud and Grace was told to think about them and to concentrate on the apparition. Everyone sat still for a few moments, listening to a grandfather clock tick away, while Grace tried to find the answers.

Dewey: Who are you?

Grace: My name is Agnes.

Dewey: Why are you here?

Grace: I'm trapped here.

Dewey: How did your physical body die?

Grace: I died somewhere outside.

Dewey: How long have you been here?

Grace: Since the late 1800s.

Dewey: Grace, can you see the woman's face?

Grace: She has dark brown eyes, thin features, gray hair.

Dewey: Describe her size.

Grace: She is short to average height and weighs about a hundred and twenty to a hundred and forty pounds.

Dewey: Now describe her clothing.

Grace: Her dress is floor-length, sort of a blue color, with a high neckline with lace around the collar.

Dewey: Was she wearing any kind of shoes or boots?

Grace: Her shoes were black and seemed to have a small heel.

Dewey: Was she wearing a wedding ring or any kind of jewelry?

Grace: She had on one ring that had stones in it.

Dewey: How old did she seem to be?

Grace: In her late fifties.

At this point, Dewey started to ask Grace if she had any knowledge of the sacrificial rites that supposedly were held in the valley between the mountains. Suddenly Grace started to sob uncontrollably. Dewey stopped the line of questioning and calmed Grace down, finally bringing her out of the trance and back to her normal self. The investigation revealed some answers, but not many.

The Herberts are still living in the house that they both felt had been their home before . . . in some other time, perhaps. They are now very accustomed to the little irregularities that occur every now and then. They have learned to live in harmony with their uninvited guest, and so far the ghost apparently feels the same way.

# The Winchester Mystery House

Sarah Pardee Winchester is certainly one of the strangest figures in California history. When her husband, William Wirt Winchester—the "Rifle King" of the nineteenth century—died in the 1880s, he left Sarah a fortune. She shouldn't have had to worry about anything again. But Sarah Winchester did little else but worry . . . about ghosts.

The Winchester fortune, accumulated by the manufacture and sale of firearms, was a constant source of guilt to Sarah. How many thousands died because of the Winchester repeating rifles? What became of the spirits of the dead Indians, soldiers, even animals, that were slaughtered? Sarah worried that her husband's soul had been confronted by the souls of his victims, and she worried about the fate of her own soul as well.

She was convinced her fortune was cursed. After her husband's funeral, Sarah consulted a spiritualist medium in Boston, who confirmed her worst fears. Sarah was told that both good and evil spirits surrounded her. The trick was to confound the bad ones and attract the good ones by providing a "haunting space" more conducive to a better class of ghosts.

Sarah hired twenty-two carpenters to work on the house and a battery of Japanese gardeners to maintain a concealing hedge around the property. And work they did—for the next forty years.

The sounds of construction never ceased, day and night, Christmas and other holidays. The house grew into a kind of dementedly inspired barracks for disembodied denizens. (By the time Sarah died, the house grew from 8 rooms to 148.) The bizarre architectural conceptions came from late-night séances Sarah conducted herself. Clothed in robes festooned with occult symbols, Sarah would sit, usually from just before midnight until two in the morning and await instructions from the dead.

They demanded endless rooms, balconies, foyers, staircases, and chimneys. Additions were built, rooms without windows or doors were fashioned, stairways leading abruptly to ceilings were installed. The spirits seemed to enjoy making their exits up fireplaces, and Sarah did her best to oblige them. Some forty-seven fireplaces and chimneys were contructed, some never rising quite to the roof.

She was also told that the departed did not care for mirrors, so in the entire sprawling series of strange rooms there are only two mirrors—one in her bathroom and one in her bedroom.

Punctuality seems important to those who have passed on. A proper haunting, as everyone knows, should begin no earlier than midnight and peak around two in the morning. Since most specters are unadorned with wristwatches, Sarah Winchester obliged them by building a belltower containing a gigantic bell. No access was provided to the bell—the inside of the tower was a sleek, unscalable wall. A rope hung from the bell to the floor, which was accessible only through a secret labyrinth, where one of the servants would ring the bell precisely at midnight, one A.M., and two A.M. The bell ringer carried an expensive watch equipped with three state-of-the-art chronometers. He would telephone the astronomical observatory every day to corroborate the times on his watch. For years Sarah's neighbors puzzled as to why the bell rang only at these three hours in the dead of night.

Sarah seemed most concerned with incubi (demon lovers), elementals (nature spirits), and the ghosts of American Indians. It's not known if these fears were instilled in her by the Boston medium she originally consulted. But it was known that her husband's gun business focused on the U.S. Army, western settlers, and Indian fighters, who undoubtedly killed thousands of Native Americans.

It was of paramount importance to keep these spirits out of her séance room, where Sarah held her meetings with the more reasonable class of phantoms. The only entrance to the room was a labyrinth of stupendous length with adjoining rooms and hallways, no doubt to entice the ghosts into making wrong turns. Push-button panels would open and she could suddenly move from one compartment to another, the secret door closing quickly behind her to leave behind all but the most nimble spooks. From the final compartment she would enter the séance room, not through a door but through a window that opened on to the top of a flight of stairs, which went down one story only to meet another flight of stairs coming back up. This was an evasion technique to discourage weary ghosts.

In fact, a maze of stairs runs through the house, many leading nowhere at all. One stairway consists of seven flights with forty-four steps—but since each step is only two inches high, the staircase is only seven feet high.

The number thirteen recurs in almost every aspect of the

house. Most windows have thirteen panes, the walls thirteen panels, thirteen steps to most flights of stairs, thirteen squares of wood in the floor, thirteen concrete squares in the driveway. The greenhouse bears thirteen cupolas; the chandeliers have thirteen globes.

Besides the many chandeliers, there are bracket lights in the walls as well as in the floors and ceilings. Sarah had hundreds of candlesticks, candles, and gas jets everywhere—even a private gas plant to feed them. The light was not to chase away the bad spirits but to accommodate the benevolent ones.

Sarah Winchester had yet another odd quirk: Her servants were not allowed to look upon her face. Once, when by mistake she encountered two of her staff who then saw her face, she fired them both, giving them a year's pay. Only her butler and secretary were allowed to see her.

After Sarah's death, it appears that her own spirit joined the many still in the house. People have heard chains rattling, whispering, and footsteps. Doorknobs turn by themselves; windows and doors open by ghostly hands. Visitors feel unexplained gusts of icy wind and cold spots. The editor of this book, Sharon Jarvis, toured the Winchester House, and upon entering the séance room she immediately felt a freezing coldness, which was not felt in any of the other 147 rooms!

Strangest of all are the balls of red light some people have seen floating through the house. When approached, these large balls of light explode.

The Winchester Mystery House is a multi-acre oddity located at 525 South Winchester Boulevard in San Jose, California. It is just off I-280.

# The Headless Horseman

One of the most haunted places in New York state's Hudson Valley is the tiny town of Kinderhook, located approximately twenty miles south of Albany. The name means "Children's Corner" in Dutch. Appropriately enough, it was in Kinderhook that Washington Irving gathered material for his classic tale, "The Legend of Sleepy Hollow."

Kinderhook and Tarrytown have always feuded over the inspiration for Irving's story of a headless horseman. The fact is, Irving created characters based on real people he knew in Kinderhook, and placed them in a Tarrytown setting.

The tall, thin schoolteacher Ichabod Crane was based on Jesse Merwin, a real teacher who was long and lanky. He taught in a little white one-room schoolhouse nestled near what is now Route 9H.

Not far down the road stands the Van Alen house, a fine example of old Dutch architecture. During Merwin's time, Katrina Van Alen lived in that house. In Irving's story, she became Katrine Van Tassel, whom Ichabod Crane unsuccessfully tried to woo.

Another character, Brom Bones, was actually Abraham Van Alstyne. The Van Alstynes are still a powerful and respected Kinderhook family, although the portrayal of Brom in the story is not exactly flattering. Apparently he was a rough, boisterous fellow given to much practical joking, especially at the schoolmaster's expense.

Lastly, the famed headless horseman seemed to have had its origins in an ancient Dutch legend that Irving simply transplanted to America. The horseman was the ghost of a Hessian soldier whose head was blown off by a cannonball. He rode the countryside in search of his head, astride a black horse that spewed fire.

But the tradition of the headless horseman still lives and is carried on to this day. During the Halloween season, someone in the village—no one really knows who—dresses up as the horseman and rides through the streets at night. However, there are reports that sometimes the imitation headless horseman had the misfortune to meet the real one, for the fright of a lifetime.

The Van Alen House, built in 1737 and now a museum, is faithfully described by Irving. Within the last decade, people who live near the house claim they have seen schoolteacher Jesse Merwin, at the stroke of midnight, gallop his horse along Route 9H and onto the drive of the Van Alen house. Merwin rides as far as a pine tree near the pond in front of the house, whereupon he suddenly disappears. It is said that ghosts have difficulty crossing water.

Washington Irving wrote "The Legend of Sleepy Hollow" while staying at Lindenwald, the home of Martin Van Buren, who was the eighth president of the United States. Van Buren was born and is buried in nearby Kinderhook and lived most of his life there (where he became the central figure in many of Kinderhook's most colorful ghost stories).

Lindenwald is just down the road from the Van Alen house. Located on twelve acres just south of Kinderhook, the sprawling estate served as Van Buren's home after he left the presidency. His ghost is the one most often seen there, usually gliding through the pine trees behind the house. But the entire house is said to have a repertoire of things that go bump in the night.

Lindenwald is a thirty-two-room Georgian-style brick mansion and is a national historic site recently restored by our national parks system. It is also one of the many haunted houses associated with the memory of Aaron Burr, the third U.S. vice president, at the turn of the nineteenth century.

Lindenwald was built in 1797 by Judge Peter Van Ness, which is where the connection to Aaron Burr begins. The judge's son Billy acted as Burr's second in Burr's infamous duel with Alexander Hamilton. The very popular Hamilton was killed in that duel, and Burr was forced to go into hiding. Many have assumed that he spent that time at Lindenwald.

Rumor has it that a mysterious secret attic room was found in the house early in the twentieth century. The owner at that time, Dr. Bascom H. Birney, was making repairs in the house and supposedly uncovered a tiny room with no outside window or inside door and which adjoined an unflattering Italian-style belltower that Van Buren had tacked onto the house. A calling card with Burr's name engraved on it was said to have been discovered inside the sealed chamber, along with a rocking chair and a carved wooden figure of a pig. This brings forth a mental image of Aaron Burr as a virtual prisoner, sitting and rocking away while he whittled to pass the time.

An article in the October 29, 1978, edition of the *Albany Times Union* quoted Jeanne Akers, whose family owned Lindenwald for forty years. While growing up in Lindenwald, Jeanne and her parents were often awakened by the strains of violin music in the wee hours of the morning. Aaron Burr was said to be an accomplished violinist. Jeanne Akers also frequently heard footsteps in the house but saw no one. Sometimes she thought it might be the ghost of Aaron Burr, but she also thought there was more than one ghost.

"Aaron Burr was reportedly something of the rough type," she said. "The ghost we knew was more a kind gentle sort, which makes me believe it was John Van Buren coming back to check the old homestead."

John was one of Martin Van Buren's sons, who was buried at sea.

But there might also be a third ghost. Visitors to Lindenwald have often reported seeing a gentleman dressed in eighteenth-century clothing wandering down the garden path. Could it be Judge Peter Van Ness, who built Lindenwald?

In the early 1980s, workers who restored Lindenwald for the National Trust saw and heard many strange things that could not be explained . . . but they wouldn't go on record with their statements. And now that the mansion is a historic site, tour guides will show you around for free—but they are advised by the management not to mention any ghosts. When a tour guide is asked about possible hauntings, he or she is likely to smile and evade the question.

Perhaps the only way to find out about ghosts is to go to Lindenwald and see for yourself.

# The Williamsburg Wraith

In May 1987, Beatrice Fensten rented an apartment on South Second Street in the Williamsburg section of Brooklyn, New York. Beatrice knew that Driggs Avenue and South Second Street was the worst section in the neighborhood with drug dealers, constant loud noises, and a steady stream of prostitutes making their way down the middle of the street early in the morning after a night's work.

But Beatrice needed a place to live, and she liked the five-room apartment. It was the top floor of an old building right on the corner. It was very bright and airy, with windows on three sides. And most of all, it was hers.

When Beatrice first looked at the apartment, everything seemed bright, even promising, despite the immediate neighborhood. The day after she signed the lease, Beatrice moved in. She knew right then and there that something was wrong . . . but it was too late to back out.

Beatrice had the strange feeling that one of the five rooms just wasn't right. It was a small corner room, off the main rooms. Yet this was the room in which Beatrice chose to sleep. After she moved in, she continually heard the sound of someone walking back and forth through all the rooms. Every night, just as she was falling asleep, the walking sounds began. At first she thought the footsteps came from the apartment below—the only other tenant in the building. Then the pounding began—fierce, sharp blows that had an incredible force and anger behind them. The pounding went on for days, and they always seemed to happen just as she was falling asleep. Though the sounds came from her dining room, which she also used as a painting studio, Beatrice thought it might be her neighbor. But she could never catch him in the act of making the sounds.

She decided to conduct an experiment, to see where the pounding might be coming from. She asked a friend to go outside and bang on the hallway walls with all his might, while she waited in the bedroom. The experiment confirmed her worst fears: The sound was coming from *inside* her apartment.

A few days later the phone rang. The woman who was the previous occupant of the apartment wanted the return of the expensive window gates she'd installed. Beatrice was all too happy to give them back because she hated the window gates; they made her feel like she was in prison.

When the woman arrived to retrieve her gates, Beatrice took the opportunity to question her. "Have you ever found anything strange in the place, like a ghost, for instance?"

Instead of laughing, the woman said, "I didn't. But I'm not really sensitive to those kinds of things." Then she added, "But my boyfriend is. He's Puerto Rican and also from this neighborhood. When he first visited me in this apartment, he became very upset and told me there was evil present."

The woman went on to relate how her boyfriend left the

apartment and returned with some blessed palms in the shape of a crucifix. He placed them around the apartment because she needed protection.

Beatrice was not surprised to learn this. She was even pleased. It meant that she was not losing her mind.

A few weeks later, Beatrice had to deal with a terrible tragedy. On May 23, her sister put a gun to her head and took her own life, leaving behind a very young son.

Beatrice's grief was compounded by the "ghost." The pounding continued, stronger than ever. A picture hanging on the kitchen wall had to be constantly straightened. One day a foul odor like rotten meat permeated the bathroom. At night she would hear what sounded like dripping coming from the air beside her head as she lay in bed. And Beatrice was sure that someone—a man—was watching her.

She asked her boyfriend Tim to stay over. They had just fallen asleep when they were both awakened by something Beatrice thought she'd never hear in her life: the sound of rattling chains, followed by a deep, agonizing moan! They sat bolt upright in bed and looked at each other, hardly believing their ears. Tim got out of bed and checked the apartment—nothing unusual was there.

The next morning Beatrice moved her bed out of the little room, angry and upset. "I'm the one that is alive," she told the empty air. "I'm supposed to be here. This is my place."

She refused to leave. Sometimes she wondered if the things that happened could be attributed to her sister's death; but the ghost had been there before her sister died. Eventually Beatrice began to get used to the ghost.

One night she was watching a little five-inch television her father had given her. Suddenly she sensed the ghost walking through the door. It came into the room and sat down on the bed between her and the television. The ghost had the misty, transparent outline of a man. It looked straight at Beatrice while she looked through it at the television. She got the distinct feeling that the ghost felt sorry for her, as though it knew the agony she was going through.

As time went on, Beatrice continued to coexist with the ghost, and odd things continued to happen. One night she was twirling the dial of her stereo, looking for a radio station, when something made her look up. She looked just in time to see the lower part of a leg take a very lively step into the kitchen. It was smoky, white, and transparent. It only showed the bottom part of a bare leg below the knee, as though the ghost did not want to be fully seen. But this seemed to be an educational lesson for Beatrice. She had always understood that there were other dimensions and extended realities. One school of thought is that ghosts are a kind of tape recording of an event, one usually charged with extreme emotions, and that the tape plays over and over again.

Perhaps the ghost was just going about its business and she had nothing to fear from it. She had always felt the ghost could never hurt her physically. But it *was* interfering with her dreams. The final straw came during a very vivid nightmare. She dreamed that she was being pursued by state policemen. For some reason, she was on the run with a criminal of some kind. As the dream progressed, they were about to be caught.

She dreamed that a state policeman stood over her, holding a double-barreled shotgun to her forehead. She could hear the sirens of the police cars and frantic voices using walkie-talkies. The dream was incredibly real, and looking up at the armed policeman, she realized she was about to die.

Then the telephone rang. Shaking, Beatrice told her friend, "You just saved my life."

The friend had casually called to say hello. Beatrice was

never so glad to be woken up. Later that morning, she remembered a clear impression of someone standing over her while she was dreaming. Not the policeman—but the ghost.

Not long after the dream, Beatrice moved out of the apartment. The ghost did not come with her. A friend suggested that perhaps the ghost misses her now that she'd gone. The thought sends a hellish chill down her spine.

# Mystery Hill

O f all the mysterious sights in the United States, Mystery Hill is probably one of the biggest. It is an ancient ruin-strewn hill covering many acres in North Salem, New Hampshire. Since controversy still rages over what this huge complex is and who built it, its current owner, Robert Stone, gave it the cryptic name.

And there are more unanswered questions: Why wasn't it until 1907 that someone actually wrote about the strange site? Why was it that until well after World War II excavations at the site to try to determine its origins always seemed to be botched, even though they were done by professional archaeologists? Where is the house on the hill that burned down during the 1800s? Not even its foundation can be located. And why did all kinds of bizarre rumors spring up about the former owners, the Pattee family?

Ninth-century Irish monks, Phoenician traders, and pre-Christian Celtic colonists have all been given the credit for building the numerous stone chambers, buildings, walls, and standing stones that are all part of Mystery Hill.

David Stewart-Smith is a master stone mason who has been the main excavator of Mystery Hill. He discovered, in the process of working on the site, that the structures had been worked on only by individuals using stone tools. In fact, the hill is littered with small stones that were obviously shaped so they could be used as tools. In addition, there have been hundreds of little stone pieces found with odd markings on them that no one has been able to interpret.

"If nothing else," says Stewart-Smith, "this tells us that none of the cultures that were supposed to have built Mystery Hill [Phoenicians, Celts, Irish Monks] could have done it, because they all had developed metal tools by the time they were supposed to have reached the site."

Experts who have worked on the site for decades now share the theory that Mystery Hill is largely a product of a Native American culture that vanished long before the coming of British settlers to New England. The only artifacts found on the site that can be positively identified are either American Indian or colonial. Scientists had found it impossible to believe that North American Indians had either the skills or resources to build large structures and maintain them for prolonged periods of time. However, recent discoveries have disproved that theory.

The discovery and excavation of Indian mounds in the Midwest made scientists realize that early North American Indians were quite capable of building large structures. Archaeologists also found that a mound-building culture existed in Maine at least two thousand years ago, consisting of people who apparently had little or no connection to the mound-building cultures that developed in the Mississippi Valley.

Archaeologists also discovered an extensive seagoing culture based in Maine and in Canada's maritime provinces which existed at least five thousand years ago. Closer to Mystery Hill has been the unearthing of the remains of an

Indian society in the Narragansett Bay area of Rhode Island that indicated the people went fishing for tuna in the open sea. Such an endeavor would need a large and sophisticated society to support it.

The area of North Salem itself is rife with thousands of Indian artifacts and many other signs of dense Indian populations after the Ice Age. Colonial records testify to the huge Indian villages dominating the area from Massabesic Lake in the north to Rye Beach in the east.

But did the Indians have the skill to work with stone? Dan Leary, a well-known New Hampshire archaeologist, pointed out that "New England Indians had a well-deserved reputation as stone masons and the colonials frequently used them as masons. The Narragansetts of Rhode Island were famous for their stone forts. The stone work done at Mystery Hill was certainly within the capabilities of any New England tribe."

According to David Stewart-Smith, the stone structures at Mystery Hill are rather sophisticated. "Megalithic structures in Europe are anchored in the soil. At Mystery Hill, most of the structures are actually closely fitted into sockets carved into the bedrock."

Much of the hill's bedrock was always exposed to the elements. There was no topsoil in which to anchor a megalithic structure, forcing the builders to take extra steps.

With the experts now leaning toward the theory of Native American builders, the controversy has moved from *who* to *when* the whole complex was actually built. Some say four thousand years ago; some say two thousand. Stewart-Smith leans toward a more recent origin. He feels the stone structures do not show the kind of weathering that four thousand years would bring.

The next unanswered question is, what was Mystery Hill used for?

It definitely is an astronomical calendar similar to Stonehenge in England. There are outer rings of stones, surrounding the many buildings, over which the sun, moon, and stars rise. Specific and important days of the calendar can be marked according to certain stones. As for the rest of Mystery Hill, the argument continues.

Was Mystery Hill a city? Was it a temple or religious site? A gigantic stone slab with a circular groove around the edge is thought to be a sacrificial altar. Was it built for one purpose but over the centuries used in other ways?

During the nineteenth century, bits and pieces of stone from the site were sold to neighboring cities to provide foundations for streets and roads. On the other hand, the site was also used during that time for occult purposes.

Mystery Hill is littered with hundreds of small stones with peculiar markings. Elmer Hinton, a senior researcher at Mystery Hill, believes that "the markings found on many of these stones were consistent with the kind of shorthand used by members of European occult societies."

Modern historians have discovered that the existence of secret occult societies was widespread in seventeenth- and eighteenth-century Europe, especially in Britain. And despite the propensity of New England Puritans to burn witches, many of their leaders and scholars had a strong interest in the occult. Such a megalithic site as Mystery Hill would be a natural attraction for colonists interested in the occult, and its distance from Puritan authorities in Boston would protect its visitors from uninvited eyes.

Dan Leary would take it even further: "I believe that it may be possible that most of the Mystery Hill structures, including those stones used to indicate solar and lunar calendars, were constructed by European alchemists between 1660 and 1700 A.D."

Leary bases his theory on the fact that during that time,

many wealthy colonial businessmen actively sponsored expeditions to look for mineral deposits in New England. Despite their occult orientation, European alchemists were the largest group of people trained to locate and identify mineral deposits. So Leary thinks they were brought to New England by various merchants to work as prospectors. Leary readily admits that at this time he has no documentary evidence to prove that powerful Puritan families such as the Leveretts and the Saltonstells brought in alchemists. However, records from that time period complain about non-British Europeans who suddenly appeared and disappeared from towns.

Nor does Leary have any direct evidence to show that Mystery Hill was built by European alchemists. However, much of the masonry material used in Mystery Hill seems to be of the same type and composition as found in Europe. If the site was built by American Indians over a long period of time, then there would be striking differences with the masonry material at different locations on the hill.

Leary says, "The calendar systems set up at Mystery Hill indicate a society that was very familiar with both the lunar and solar calendars. Yet we don't find cruder, less sophisticated complexes in other parts of New England to indicate a society learning about the solar and lunar years." The implication is that Mystery Hill was built by people who didn't have to experiment because they already knew how to do it.

"Mystery Hill is a unique site and it really shouldn't be," Leary declares. "That is why I think it's possible for Mystery Hill to have been built by a group of individuals, such as European alchemists, who were already familiar with both the lunar and solar calendars. As for the stone work, there were many Indian stone masons they could have hired to do the work."

When historian Scott Green visited Mystery Hill to research

this story, he felt surrounded by a somber eeriness even on a bright fall day. The site *does* have an odd feeling about it. No wonder it inspired some of the most horrifying settings in the works of H. P. Lovecraft, an American master of horror fiction.

Mystery Hill, located just off Route 111, is open to the public on weekends in April and November, and daily from May through October.

# The Show Must
# Go On

It was late one April evening in 1988, when Rob Riley knelt onstage, paint can at his elbow. He stared at the flats—background canvases for a play—that were spread over the auditorium of the Broken Arrow Community Playhouse. He'd already spent two hours painting them, but it seemed there were just as many as when he started. But painting flats was part of the job. At age twenty-five Riley had been acting for nearly nine years. His interests went beyond just acting, his enthusiasm extending to everything from set design to lighting to even painting scenery flats. As he painted, Riley reflected on the many good times he'd had in the small playhouse. Some of the best had been when he worked with Bob Plumb, the founder of the playhouse. Plumb had directed Riley in *Fiddler on the Roof* when Riley had been only sixteen years old. He'd learned a lot from Bob Plumb, who, like Riley, was involved in every aspect of theatrical work necessary to produce a play.

*I sure could use some help from him right now,* thought Riley.

As Riley diligently continued, he couldn't shake the feeling that he wasn't alone in the theater. But he was. Nobody but him was scheduled to be there that evening, and the side doors were locked, so no one could have sneaked in. The front doors were unlocked, but they were large and difficult to open without making lots of noise.

When he couldn't shake the feeling that he had company, Riley looked out over the audience seats. He saw a familiar figure in the high seats, near the control booth. It was Bob Plumb, sitting there with his arms and legs crossed. Bob was dressed in what had become his uniform over the years: a brown tam, gold cup suspenders, brown pants, and a yellow shirt.

Riley started to say "Hi, Bob," but suddenly stopped. An awful realization hit him. He stood, quickly cleaned and stored the paintbrushes, and fled the theater under the watchful eyes of Bob Plumb—who had been dead for over eight years.

That Bob Plumb's spirit still hangs around the small community theater in Broken Arrow, Oklahoma, is no surprise to Tom Berenson, another local actor.

"He loved that place and spent as much time as he could there," Berenson told reporter Bradley Sinor. "There might not be a community theater if it hadn't been for Bob Plumb."

Plumb had always loved the theater. Down South, he'd managed a dinner theater. Later he ran a community theater in Lawton. In Broken Arrow, he was a public schoolteacher but devoted all his spare time to the community theater there.

While most people knew Plumb as a bright, cheerful person, there was another side to the man. Every day of his life Bob battled an emotional disability—schizophrenia. Eventually the darker side of his personality had won out.

Shortly before his death, Plumb walked up to Berenson and genially patted him on the head during a wrap party. (The playhouse cast and crew were celebrating a successful run of *The Creature Creeps*.) "He was so calm and quiet that I never suspected a thing," said Berenson. "I realize now that he had apparently decided what to do and was winding things down.

"One day, Bob borrowed a friend's van and backed it up on his lawn. He then ran a hose from the exhaust to a bedroom window. He went inside and let the carbon monoxide fumes do the work he intended them to do."

The night of Plumb's death, several of the people he'd worked with on the theater board had reported strange incidents. They all saw doors opening by themselves. They felt a strange breeze when there couldn't be one. And they had the feeling that someone was staring at them.

"It was almost like Plumb was telling them that the theater was in their hands now," said Berenson.

For several years after his death, a painting of Bob Plumb hung in the theater office. Because of the manner of his death, occasionally people would object to the painting and remove it. Without telling anyone or asking permission, they'd take down the painting and put it away in storage.

"My wife, Sandy, was working for the theater at the time," said Berenson. "Within a few days of the disappearance of the painting, she'd walk into the office and find it back on the wall."

Most people who knew about these incidents felt that the picture was being replaced by Plumb's friends. But no one ever came forward to claim responsibility for doing it. A few suspected that it was Plumb himself, thumbing his nose at his detractors. Tom Berenson continued to work at the playhouse. One day he was in the office when the manager walked in, white as a sheet. "I think you better take a look at this," she told him unsteadily.

She handed Berenson a card—one of the cards people

filled out when they wanted to volunteer their services at the playhouse. And the playhouse needed all the volunteers it could get.

Berenson stared for a long time at the card, which had been filled out by a young man. "Is this a joke?" he finally asked.

"No, he's right outside. Call him in and talk to him yourself."

A young man in his late twenties came in. He had recently moved to Broken Arrow. He admitted he'd never been involved with any kind of theatrical work. "But in the last few weeks," he said, "I've had this overwhelming urge to come down here and volunteer."

"Glad to have you on board. We can always use new help."

The young man and the manager left; Berenson stood there with the card still in his hand. The young man's address was 119 South Jackson—the same house that had been Bob Plumb's home until his death.

"Thanks, Bob," Berenson said with a chuckle, and walked out of the office.

The Broken Arrow Community Playhouse is located at 1109 East Memphis, Broken Arrow, Oklahoma. It's a one-story building in an isolated industrial area.

# Ghosts of the Oxford Bar

The Oxford Bar and Grill in Pueblo, Colorado, is a nice, cozy neighborhood bar on the main street. It is similar to the other neighborhood bars that dot the small blue-collar city in all but one unusual respect—unusual, that is, for anywhere but the Dark Zone.

The outside of the bar has heavy, leaded glass windows lit by the mandatory neon beer signs. Inside, it's always dark regardless of the time of day. The building is long and narrow, with the traditional long wooden bar. Booths and tables line the wall. In the rear of the room, a pool table and dart board are brightly lit for the various dart clubs and regular customers that frequent the bar.

Though it's a typical bar, its patrons think the Oxford Bar is special—and it is. Its regular patrons are not only in this world but in the next—like the shadowy presence that startles the bartenders or suddenly plays "Happy Birthday" on the jukebox.

Terry Vellar and his family have owned the Oxford Bar for nearly ten years, with multiple encounters with "regulars'' from the spirit world. When the family first started working the bar, long-time customers would joke that Harry, the previous owner who had recently died, would still come into the bar and play the jukebox. They said Harry had had a hard life and only seemed truly happy when in the bar.

Occasionally the jukebox would start to play ''Happy Birthday'' by itself. That was one of Harry's favorite songs, and he would make a big fuss on someone's birthday. But the Vellars were convinced that mechanical problems with the old machine were responsible and didn't think much about it at the time.

One night, after the last customer had left the bar, Terry's daughter Mary Beth turned from locking the front door. ''When I turned,'' she told reporter Nancy A. Cucci, ''I could see a man standing at the end of the bar, facing the pool table. I could see him very clearly; he was wearing work-type blue jeans and a red flannel shirt.''

Mary Beth was frightened. She knew that no one else was supposed to be in the bar, and she immediately thought he was a robber. ''But before I could call out, he turned and looked straight at me.''

He was an older man in his late sixties, with gray hair and blue eyes. ''We stared at each other for a moment,'' Mary Beth said, ''and then he disappeared.''

Mary Beth finally mentioned her experience to one of the regular customers and described what she had seen. A group of people thought they recognized him as the former owner and returned with a photo album. Sure enough, Mary Beth was able to pick out his picture and identify Harry as the stranger in the bar.

Mary Beth still sees the ghost regularly. ''He looks solid, not shadowy or transparent. You can't see through him. He looked just like any other person would, standing there, and then all of a sudden he's gone.''

Reporter Nancy A. Cucci did some research about Pueblo for her several articles about the town's ghostly goings-on. She discovered Pueblo is known as a "hot spot," an energy place which attracts spirits wanting to stay in the material world. That would explain the unusual number of ghostly sightings and paranormal occurrences there.

Pueblo is an old city dating back to pioneer days. With its dry, desertlike climate, it attracted people seeking relief from consumption, one of the major diseases of the 1800s. In later years, Pueblo was known for its tuberculosis sanatorium, but before then many people with terminal tuberculosis died along the banks of the river . . . and stayed in Pueblo.

Some of the other spirits in the Oxford Bar seem to come from this earlier time in Pueblo's history. The site of the bar is located across the street from an old pioneer graveyard, which was removed and built over before the turn of the century.

In the dark shadows near the front of the bar and behind a divider, a menacing figure that is totally dressed in black sometimes sits undisturbed by the rest of the bar's patrons. Terry Vellar described the man as wearing what appeared to be a long black raincoat—the type usually worn by gunslingers in the 1870s—and a black, broad-brimmed hat pushed over his face.

"He was solid and looked real as anyone to me," said Terry. "But I didn't notice him come in. It was eerie, seeing him just sitting there, and he gave me the chills. I was distracted for a moment, and when I looked back, he was gone."

Another ghostly regular comes in to check out the music selections in the jukebox. One early evening, Terry watched as a disheveled-looking man in his mid-twenties walked into the bar. He was dressed in a brown work shirt and looked like he had a three-day-old beard. He stood by the jukebox, just looking at it.

After a while, Terry called out to him, asking him what he wanted to drink. The man turned around, smiled, and disappeared. Terry doesn't bother to call out to him anymore.

Another visitor to the establishment is a little girl, about eight, dressed in a long white pioneer-style dress. One day, before opening the bar to customers, Terry realized that the little girl was inside, playing near the back door. He thought she was just some kid from the street who'd wandered in, though he briefly wondered how she got passed the locked doors. He watched as she skipped through the bar and then disappeared before reaching the front door.

Except for the ghost in black, the various phantoms are never threatening or frightening. The Vellars and the regular patrons have come to expect the unexpected. And more often than not, the ghosts are blamed for bad pool shots.

The Oxford Bar and Grill is located at 419 North Santa Fe Avenue. You are welcome to spend a cozy evening there, eating and drinking . . . and waiting for the ghosts to show up. But please don't ask the gunslinger if he's quick on the draw.

# Spectral Restorations

Nyack, New York, has many old houses, some dating back to the late seventeenth century. Several possess histories of haunting or paranormal occurrences. The area is proud of its supernatural heritage, flaunted via feature articles in the local newspapers and a local registry of haunted houses. On Broadway there is even a restaurant called the Coven Café. But not many people know about one particular house on Prospect Street.

The house was purchased in 1980 by Diana and Ted Carson. It was a two-family house and the Carsons intended to use it as an income-producing property. (Their own home was less than a mile away.) They rented the upstairs apartment to Diana's sister Jacqueline, who lived there with her son Jonathan and boyfriend Adam. Jackie and Adam were helping to renovate the house.

In researching the house, the Carsons discovered the earliest property transaction recorded for the site was in 1720. Diana and Ted were eager for friends and relatives to see the interior renovations aimed at restorating earlier details.

Despite the winter weather, they invited an old friend, Roberta Klein-Mendelson, who visited the house with her husband and daughter. (All the names in this story are changed with the exception of Roberta's.) Roberta noticed that the house had a peculiar upper-level porch; the facade reminded her more of French Quarter New Orleans than lower Hudson Valley. Walking up the front stairs, Roberta felt rather strange. The moment she entered the unoccupied lower level, a sudden, deep cold and an intense pressure surrounded her. She turned around and saw, superimposed over winter mud, a garden in full bloom. Without thinking, Roberta turned to Diana and said, "There are presences inhabiting the house.

"What do you mean?"

"Ghosts."

As everyone went upstairs, Diana gleefully announced, "Roberta thinks the house is haunted." Roberta was embarrassed. Diana was one of very few people she had told of her psychic abilities.

Changing the subject, Roberta informed Diana, "You really ought to put in an herb garden this spring. It would do very well."

Instead of focusing the conversation away from the supernatural, the comment had the opposite effect. Ted, Adam, Diana, and Jackie all shared a look. Then Ted said, "Interesting that you should say so. Since we moved in, I've had an overwhelming urge to plant an herb garden. I've even begun to list the seeds, and I've never been a gardener before. It's almost as if—"

"The house wants it," Roberta finished.

Ted nodded. "Tell us about these ghosts."

The children were sent off to play before Roberta would say any more. "There's not much to tell," she said when they had left. "I don't sense any evil—just a few spirits who consider this their home. Have you seen or heard anything out of the ordinary?''

''Right after we moved in, there was a lot of noise in the attic,'' said Jackie. ''We've heard footsteps up and down the stairs after we went to bed. In the last week or so it quieted down. Do you think we should do something about it?''

''That's kind of premature. Why don't we just wait? If you get uncomfortable, we can send them on their way. How about showing us the house now?''

It was as charming as Roberta had expected, although Diana was unhappy about the lower bathroom—the entrance to it faced the kitchen. She was afraid that existing pipes or wiring would preclude relocating the doorway.

Roberta blurted, ''I think you'll find there's a door in this wall that backs on to the hallway.'' But Ted was reluctant to consider tearing down the wall just on Roberta's hunch. They all toured the rest of the house and grounds, and the remainder of the visit was uneventful.

Later that week, Jackie and Adam worked to restore the old house. Jackie began stripping paint from the living room's window frames, while Adam tore plywood off a concealed fireplace. Suddenly Jackie felt a sense of approval coming from behind her. She turned and saw a ghostly couple watching. He had salt-and-pepper hair and a large mustache; she was blond, dressed in turn-of-the-century clothing. They nodded and smiled at Jackie, then faded away. By the time Adam looked up, there was nothing to see.

Later, while working alone in the living room, Adam looked up to discover he had a visitor. A man in knee britches and vest, his hair tied back in a queue, had appeared. He motioned to Adam and guided him toward the hall, where the ghost opened a door in the wall. He walked through and then ghost and door both quietly disappeared. When Adam tore down the wall, he found a wooden doorframe where Roberta had indicated. He was pleased but astonished at the supernatural assistance.

The next week Jackie was again refinishing the stripped windows when she perceived the sensation of approval. Behind her was the blond woman, smiling. Then, beside Adam, who was laying a new floor, appeared the mustached man.

"Adam, look," Jackie hissed.

Adam looked up, then behind him. He saw both ghosts, who immediately faded. The mustached man was not the figure Adam had previously seen. This meant the house had three ghostly residents!

Although the ghosts seemed benevolent, even helpful, Jackie and Adam were increasingly uncomfortable at the notion of their home being a supernatural clubhouse. They even discussed the possibility of an exorcism. However, before anything was done about the ghosts, the remodeling was finished. The apparitions ceased. The ghosts apparently were satisfied.

But then Jackie's son Jonathan started having nightmares. He refused to discuss their content, but Jackie remarked that after every nightmare his room seemed icy. They moved him into a smaller bedroom, yet the bad dreams and subsequent chill persisted. Now, during the day, Jonathan was unwilling to be out of sight of his mother while within the house.

Finally it was decided that Roberta would perform an exorcism on the night of the next new moon. Time was more than ripe to inform these entities that they were inhabiting the wrong plane. That afternoon Jackie and Adam cleaned the house thoroughly, while envisioning the removal of any negative or inappropriate vibrations. At sundown, Roberta arrived with several bunches of dried herbs from her garden. She had selected those known for their protective qualities, including rosemary, lavender, and juniper. She steeped these in hot water, then directed Jackie and Adam to sprinkle the resulting liquid throughout the house, while repeating the twenty-third psalm.

Meanwhile, Roberta inscribed pentacles of protection over each doorway and window, saying her own prayers as she worked. When the house was warded, they went to the property boundaries and sprinkled and prayed there as well. The final part of the ritual was a prayer for the safe transit and repose of those entities who had previously inhabited the house.

It was the first time Roberta had ever performed an exorcism. Not for several years did she learn how foolishly reckless she had been in performing it. It was actually a dangerous thing to do, since it could have had the opposite effect: The house on Prospect Street might have had an increase in ghostly inhabitants—or worse.

But the exorcism seemed to work, and Jonathan's bad dreams stopped. There were no more footsteps on the stairs, no more cold spots. The ghosts are quiet for now. But who knows? One day a ghostly door in the wall may open and three specters might come home.

# Europe's Denizens of the Deep

*U*lrich Magin is a reporter and foreign correspondent currently living in Germany. As a member of the International Fortean Organization (dedicated to cataloging and investigating the paranormal), he has been actively involved in investigative research. As a result, he became interested in the long tradition—and sightings—of "sea serpents" throughout many countries in Europe. A great many lakes and rivers had such "monster" traditions stretching back into antiquity:

In the first century A.D. travelers on the Rhone River, between Arles and Avignon, France, were warned about a creature that liked to swallow up passersby. The creature was called a *tarasque* and was said to look like a cross between a turtle and several other creatures. It had a scaly dragonlike body topped by a bearded face, a spiny shell, and six legs.

Legend has it that the creature was put under a spell by St. Martha, using her crucifix and holy water, so the local villagers could kill it. A statue—actually it's a float—of the *tar-*

*asque* is still shown in the town of Tarascon during its annual festival.

But the *tarasque* may not be vanquished, as previously thought. In 1954 and 1955 there were reports of "monsters" in the Rhone River. And in 1964, two tourists, father and son, saw what they described as a long-necked sea serpent.

Another monster—perhaps the same one—has been sighted in Étang de Vaccarès, a lagoon located between the mouths of the Grand Rhone and Petit Rhone rivers. If it is the same creature, it likes to travel. In 1934 an animal with long neck and small head swam in the Doubs River, which has its source in Switzerland and then flows into the Rhone. An account of the creature appeared in the *New York Herald Tribune*, which led Ulrich Magin to speculate on the possibility of a herd of Nessie-type creatures migrating up and down the rivers.

Italy has modern sightings as well as the expected legends. Lago Maggiore is said to be inhabited by a horse-headed dragon who fortunately likes to eat fish instead of people. The creature was supposedly mentioned by the novelist Stendhal at the beginning of the nineteenth century, and it was seen again in 1934 by fishermen at the mouth of the Ticino River.

Just to the west of Lago Maggiore is Lake Como, which is very similar ecologically. Both flow into the Po River. It is logical that a creature could have traveled from Maggiore to Como, so it comes as no surprise that in November 1946 fishermen saw a marine monster in Lake Como. It was described as scaly, well over thirteen feet long, and covered with red marks.

The town of Goro, which is just across the Po River from Venice, claims a monster has continually terrorized it. The creature was seen most often in the 1970s, when it came ashore several times. It was more than ten feet long and was reported as "thick as a dog." It has also been described as a large snake with legs.

Several newspaper reports in the early 1980s tell of another Italian lake monster. In March 1980, off the island of Pantelleria, a trawler had something mysterious caught in its nets. The trawler, *Socrate I*, was close to the island when a submerged object of a large size was snagged in its nets. It was widely thought they had caught a Russian submarine, but it may have been a sea serpent. Since the object was fairly deep, the crewmen could not see it. But they could feel it struggle. After several hours, the object broke through the nets and escaped.

Two years later, in 1982, something was heard making frightening noises in Venus Lake on the island of Pantelleria. Since it was nighttime, nothing could be seen. And there were no volunteers to sail out in the darkness to investigate the bizarre sounds.

On April 26, 1979, two water policemen (the equivalent of the coast guard) saw something in Zwischenahner Meer, near Bad Zwischenahn, Germany. It was about twelve feet long and had a dark slimy back. It was compared to a giant catfish. Several other sightings followed—it was even blamed for the disappearance of local dogs—and the creature was dubbed the "German Nessie."

Stories about the creature appeared as far away as the *New York Times* and the *Bangkok Post*. For a while the lake was crowded with hopeful anglers, since a twelve-foot "catfish" would be some catch! When some anglers lost their fishing lines or rods, they claimed the creature had pulled it right out of their hands. This Nessie had enough sense to stay away from the crowds and presumably went into deeper water.

Another modern sighting took place in 1982 at Lake Zeegrynski, Poland. Bathers were frightened by a twenty-foot monster with a slimy black head and rabbitlike ears. This was the first time a terrifying sea serpent was described with such a benign word. Again the creature was thought to be like a giant catfish, similar to the one in Germany.

The idea of a twelve- or twenty-foot catfish sounds a bit fishy. However, very large catfish—and sturgeons—have been caught over the years. But this would not explain the monster that inhabits Poland's Black Lake.

Legend has it that a monster has lived in the Black Lake, near Poznan, for as long as anyone can remember. Locals believe it is the incarnation of the devil because it has successfully evaded all attempts to catch it—and because fish caught in the lake are mysteriously inedible.

Despite the local legends, in the winter of 1578 a group gathered to fish in Black Lake through holes in the ice. Twice they put a net in the lake but came up empty. On the third try, they snagged something. The men hauled on the net and got the fright of their lives. Up through the ice came the head of a monster. It resembled the head of a goat with two big horns—it also had glowing red eyes. (This very much sounds like the world-famous 1975 photo of the creature in Loch Ness, Scotland, taken more than four hundred years later.)

The men dropped the net and ran for their lives. At the same time, a storm blew up and a loud roaring noise filled the forest surrounding the lake. The air became unbreathable, as though it were poisoned, and many of the men fell sick.

To Ulrich Magin's knowledge, the locals have never tried this again.

Magin's research shows lake creatures fall into two groups: giant fish and animals similar to the Loch Ness monster. North of the Alps the reports are usually of giant fish. The reports of "longnecks" seem to be localized south of the Alps, either in large alpine lakes connected to the sea by the Po River or the rivers of the Rhone Basin.

Magin feels there is not enough evidence to prove the giant

fish are other than just that. But he does believe the Po and the Rhone might have a small resident population of monsters—or the rivers might be the migratory routes to and from the Mediterranean.

You are welcome to find out for yourself.

# The Phantom of
# the Organ Loft

---

Wealthy Uriah Spray Epperson had the first car in Kansas City, Missouri. He also had the biggest house—a fifty-four-room Tudor mansion, which his wife Elizabeth called Epperson's Folly. It took several years to build at a cost of $450,000.

When the childless Eppersons moved in, they brought with them a talented house guest whom they introduced as their adopted daughter Harriet—although Harriet was ten years older than Elizabeth.

Elizabeth was a patron of the arts and Harriet supervised their musical entertainment. She designed an organ for placement in the loft of their great room, which also contained a small stage for plays. Construction of the organ continued while Harriet organized musical community projects sponsored by Uriah.

But on December 20, 1922, Harriet mysteriously died. Her death certificate attributes the cause of death to surgical shock following a gallbladder operation. There was no autopsy, nor a death notice or obituary in the local newspapers. Harriet was buried not in a plot owned by the Eppersons, but with her own family in nearby Independence. The organ was never finished.

Uriah died in 1927, wealthy, respected, and without a tinge of scandal. Elizabeth died in 1939, leaving behind the house at 5200 Cherry Street . . . and Harriet's ghost.

There were rumors that Harriet had been a little too friendly with the hired help. And even more rumors that she had died as the result of a botched abortion.

The house was inherited by a relative who tried living in it . . . for a short while. He soon gave the house to the University of Missouri in 1943; it was first used as a men's dormitory, then by the School of Education, and later as a student center. Over the years, stories grew about the house.

It wasn't until the 1970s, when the building was used by the Music Department, that Harriet's presence intensified. A ghostly piano was heard near the basement pool. Some students claimed they saw Harriet wearing an evening gown, as though ready for a recital. Sometimes they could hear her sing. Sometimes they saw her clutching a bundle in her arms (like a baby?) and cry in choked sobs.

By 1978 Harriet got tired of a student-only audience and started performing for the maintenance staff and security guards. On weekends, when the building was empty, the guards would hear footsteps when no one was there.

One security patrolman was sitting in his car at five A.M. writing a report. The patrol car was parked in the Epperson parking lot, which was made of cobblestone. His was the only car there at that time of morning, and there was no traffic. Suddenly he heard the sounds of an accident: screeching rubber, bending metal, broken glass. His patrol car was jarred and rocked. Momentarily he thought he'd been rear-ended, but when he turned his head, nothing was there. Nothing except for his own skid marks.

One of the custodians was changing a light bulb in the monstrous chandelier in the great room. He just happened to have a Bible in his pocket. As he was standing on a ladder, the chandelier suddenly, and without reason, dropped to the floor. As it passed, it bounced against the Bible. He was unhurt and the chandelier was not broken in any way; it was simply pulled back to the ceiling. No one could determine why the chandelier fell, since it could only be lowered and raised by rope.

In the fall of 1978, at about two o'clock one morning, two patrolmen were making a routine inspection of the inside of the Epperson House. As they moved from room to room, they would turn the lights on and then turn them off when they left. After their rounds, as they began to leave, a problem arose in the main entrance hall. There the light wouldn't turn off. Thinking it was stuck, they kept jiggling the switch, but the light still stayed on. The two men decided to lock up and leave the light on until maintenance could check it out later in the day. They moved down the hall and stopped so one patrolman could light a cigarette. As they stood there, about ten feet away from the switch they saw an arm in a blue coat sleeve materialize and turn the light off for them.

There have been other problems with the lights at Epperson House. A number of other officers have had the experience of going through the building at night, making sure all the lights were off, locking the house securely . . . and then finding that a light was on in the tower. What makes this so unusual is that there are no lights in the tower—no wiring, no switches, no light fixtures. Since the stairs leading to the tower have been condemned as unsafe, no one has investigated the phantom light in the tower . . . not that they want to.

After the reports about the strange doings at Epperson House began to pile up, the security chief decided to call for help. He contacted Maurice Schwalm, a well-known occult investigator in Kansas City.

On May 5, 1979, Schwalm and a small team of psychics came to the campus. After interviewing many of the witnesses of the ghostly events at the house, the team decided to form a meditation circle in an attempt to psychically link with the house. One of the members turned on a tape recorder, but had to shut it off when it began howling. Chairs squeaked loudly, although the people in them were still. They also heard the sounds of the tuning or plucking of stringed instruments.

Maurice Schwalm left the circle and walked through the building, taking photographs. When later developed, two photographs were quite unusual. One shows a candelabra, fully lit with candles. It wasn't in the room at the time—and the room was dark when Schwalm took the photo. The second picture is of a translucent red skull superimposed on the tower.

In their investigation and psychic impressions, there were the recurrent themes of pregnancy, a botched abortion, and a male employee who might have been too friendly with Harriet. But it is also possible that her abdominal complaints did not receive prompt medical attention because the Eppersons were Christian Scientists. However, one thought was clear to the psychics present that day: Harriet says she will continue to play the piano until her organ is finished.

While Harriet's performances are intriguing, apparently Schwalm's psychics are not. It was reported by the meditating psychic who sat next to Uriah Epperson's formal portrait that Mr. Epperson was less than entertained. All through the meditation, the painting was a source of snoring sounds and cigar smoke!

The last Schwalm heard of Harriet, she was most displeased

with the architectural students. In December 1987, the students were working on sketches of proposed renovations to the building. Each time they posted a sketch on the wall, Harriet would take it down. Perhaps the university would do well to include the restoration of Harriet's organ in their plans.

# The Lloyd Street Gnome

P atti and Wolfgang Stolp spent the early years of their married life in the second-floor apartment of an old duplex. The building was located at Seventy-first and Lloyd streets (two blocks south of North Avenue) in Wauwatosa, Wisconsin. They moved there in 1972 and their daughter Gena was born two years later. But the happy family of three was actually a family of four, which the Stolps didn't discover for some time. . . .

The building's owners had told the young couple that they could use any items they found in the attic. Patti discovered a set of antique lace curtains, which she hung in their dining room. She also found an old wicker basket, a small wooden chest, and some other useful articles.

Soon after the items were taken from the attic and brought into their apartment, Wolfgang noticed areas of the building where there were strange changes in temperature. The most affected areas were the nursery, the attic, the cellar, and the back hallway, where French doors separated the hall from the rest of the apartment.

192

"As we walked through the living room, into the dining room, and to the hall at the back, near the bedrooms," Wolfgang told reporter Gail Larson Toerpe, "the temperature went from warm to hot to cold and back to warm."

In the cellar were deep cracks and broken sections of flooring. One section of the concrete was shaped like a square and was raised above the others. Each time the Stolps went into the cellar, the square piece seemed to have risen higher. Even Patti's visiting sister Sharon took a dislike to the cellar, which always seemed too dark and too cold to her. In the apartment, pictures were found tilted in the morning, though Wolf or Patti had straightened them the night before. Sugar bowls and other small items were tipped over. And other objects which no one had moved were found out of their normal places.

There were days when Patti was alarmed by the strange sounds baby Gena made in the nursery. During nap time, when Gena was asleep, something would awaken her. Patti would hear odd gasping sounds. Upon entering the nursery, she'd find the baby standing up, dazedly staring at the ceiling.

Wolfgang, who worked second shift at the time, often stayed up till the early hours of the morning. "Sometimes I'd sit and paint flowers on boxes or paint pictures of children," he said. "Sometimes I did macramé—I was going through my 'hippie' stage." Reporter Toerpe had a hard time visualizing the tall, distinguished-looking man in this way. Wolfgang went on to explain that each night it was his habit to light candles throughout the house.

Sitting in the silence of the flickering candles, Wolfgang's solitude was occasionally disturbed by a shock of heat—an indescribable wave of "electric energy" that rushed through his body. On one such night, as Wolf sat amid wavering shadows, he realized he could see a shadow move! It darted around the apartment. Pictures and small furniture were displaced as the shadow rushed around the rooms and into the nursery, where it disappeared.

Wolfgang was stunned and could only hope he had imagined it. But the next morning, when he saw the furniture and pictures were out of place, he knew it was real. The darting silhouette appeared on a number of evenings, and as always, it ended up in the baby's room.

Eventually the shadow coalesced into a figure. One night, surrounded by candlelight, something made Wolfgang look up. Down the hall, behind the French doors, was the hazy image of a little man, about two and a half feet tall. The large, luminous eyes of the diminutive man peered through the paneled windows of the door.

Wolfgang rose from this chair and walked cautiously toward the doors. As Wolfgang drew closer, the small man darted into the nursery and disappeared. Wolfgang looked back at the paneled window and could see the vapor of breath marks still left on the glass.

One night in 1974, Patti's sister Sharon was baby-sitting for them. The Stolps had never told her about any of the apartment's weird incidents, so Sharon was completely unprepared for what happened that evening. While sitting in the living room, she felt a cold, creepy chill come over her, accompanied by a sense of urgency to check on the baby.

The nursery was dimly lit by a small night light. Sharon didn't hear any noise, but still she was hesitant to enter the room. A shadowy figure caught her eye.

"I saw a small gnomelike man, dancing in the corner near the crib. He was about as tall as a two-year-old child. He was dressed in Old World clothing: knee-length britches, suspenders or a vest—I couldn't tell which in the dim light—over a loose-fitting shirt. He had longish hair, a mustache, and a beard, and was unkempt. It looked like a caricature of the little gnome faces one sees in curio shops."

Incredulous and frightened, Sharon never turned her back or took her eyes off the queer little creature in the corner. Walking slowly to the crib, she picked up the sleeping baby and cautiously backed out the door. She spent the rest of the night huddled in the living room. From that time on, when she baby-sat again, it was with another person accompanying her and with all the lights on in the apartment.

When Wolfgang described the experiences to his German-born mother, she explained that the gnome he saw was not uncommon in her European upbringing. She suggested that the creature's habitat in the attic may have been disturbed when the curtains and other items were taken out and brought downstairs. She also recommended a solution.

Wolfgang followed her advice and so one morning Patti awoke to find salt all over the floor. As she vacuumed it up, her husband shouted at her to leave it alone. He had put the salt down according to his mother's instruction. Later he swept it up, took it to work, and burned it in fire.

Burned salt and prayers are thought to be ways to get rid of aberrations like the Lloyd Street gnome. The young couple also hung a crucifix in the baby's room.

Within a month it appeared as though the salt had worked. The gnome wasn't seen again and the strange incidents stopped. But the little man was not forgotten. When Gena was around three years old, the Stolps took her to visit an aunt. The aunt wanted to show them something she'd just bought—an unusual and fairly large gnomelike doll. Gena screamed and her mother says that to this day Gena still hates to look at gnomes.

Years passed, and by 1990 the family no longer lived in the apartment. The Stolps had three more children and needed larger living quarters, which they found in a house at Forty-sixth and Meineke streets, one block north of North Avenue. Sixteen-year-old Gena got her own bedroom on the first floor.

That year the family decided to have a rummage sale. Gena helped gather the items together, which included the old wicker basket and other things from their original apartment.

Digging up these items from the past apparently disturbed the gnome, because odd things started happening in Gena's bedroom. She always slept with a fan on. But in the morning she'd find the fan turned off.

One night, while Gena was at her desk studying, she glimpsed something dark flitting about the room. She looked up to see a small, shadowy form about two and a half feet high darting by.

Had the little man nested in the wicker basket, with delicate lace curtains as his cover? Or had the chest been his home all these years? And it's too soon to know if the gnome has returned for good—he seems to prefer visiting Gena—or if his dwelling place was sold at the rummage sale. So if you've bought an antique basket or chest lately in Wauwatosa, we suggest you stop at the local supermarket and stock up on salt.

# Lawton's Elusive Light

"**I**f you ask me, this 'ghost' thing sounds more like an excuse to get a girl out to some dark country road," Sue Sinor said.

Her husband, Brad, turned to her and chuckled. "Now, I never said it was a ghost! This is just a strange light that people have been seeing. But it wouldn't surprise me in the slightest to know that some guy had done just that."

"Like you or your friend Steve?"

"*Moi!* Would I have done something like that?" Brad said with mock indignation.

The couple was en route from their home in northeastern Oklahoma to Lawton, where Brad had lived most of his life. This would be their first return to the area since their wedding there two months earlier. Located in southwestern Oklahoma, Lawton was founded in the early 1900s as the last portions of the old Indian Territory were being opened to white settlement.

To pass the time during their five-hour drive, Brad told his bride some of Lawton's strange legends: the glowing tombstone, the bridge where the spirits of the dead could be heard crying into the darkness, and even the old man who in the 1940s claimed to be Jesse James. The thing that intrigued Sue the most was the story of the strange old church just west of town.

"The first time that I can remember hearing about it was when I was working out at the drive-in," Brad said. "The old church is abandoned, has been for years. But if you go out there late at night, they say that you can still see a light glowing in the sanctuary."

Depending on who was telling the story, the church had been used by Catholics, Baptists, fundamentalists, or even Satanists. What had gone on inside varied with who was telling the story. That there were as many different versions of the facts as there were people to tell them was no great surprise, any more than the fact that the old church had been a magnet for thrill-seeking teenagers for decades.

Later on, in Lawton, they talked to Brad's friend about the church.

"It *is* haunted, if that's what you would call that light," Steve Meade said.

Steve poured himself another beer from the pitcher that sat on the table between the Sinors and himself. He had worked with Brad off and on for a dozen years at the Hankin's Drive-In Theater, first as concessionist, then projectionist, and finally as co-assistant manager.

"I still think that it sounds more like an excuse to get a girl out to a dark country road on a Saturday night," said Sue.

Steve laughed. "Seriously, though, it's real. I've been out there and seen it too many times to fall for some sort of joke. Besides, it's been going on for too long—my stepfather told me about seeing it when *he* was a teenager."

"Are you sure that it isn't just a light somebody forgot to turn off?" asked Brad.

"There hasn't been electricity to the place in more than thirty years," said Steve. "And before you ask, there's no chance that it's headlights reflecting in the windows. All the glass was broken out of them years ago."

At Sue's urging, the three of them decided to visit the old church that night. While the church was now within the corporate city limits of Lawton, when it was first built the new city had been barely more than a few hastily erected buildings and a lot of tents.

The church looked like many others from the turn of the century: a single building with a steeple, from where the cast-iron bell would have echoed out the summons to Sunday morning worship, and a large pair of double doors in the front.

A rusty wrought-iron fence surrounded the property. Yet here and there designs were still visible in the metal: circles, quarter moons, and doves. Off to the east they could see the familiar glow of city lights. To the west was darkness, and all around them were the sounds of the wind across the Oklahoma prairie.

"There are people who say that this proves the place was a Satanist church," Steve said, pointing to the various emblems.

Sue shook her head in disgust. "Good grief, that is about as stupid as saying Proctor & Gamble's symbol is Satanic."

If there had ever been a lock on the building, it had long since been pulled off. When the doors were opened, their ancient hinges creaked. Inside were some plain wooden benches that had served as pews. Most of them had long since rotted away, though one or two still stood. Here and there were signs of other, more recent visitors: a crumpled page of the local newspaper, crushed fast-food packages, and empty beer cans.

As it grew progressively nearer to midnight, they left the church and walked back to the car. Sue sat in the car with the door open, while her husband and his friend nervously paced about, making bad jokes and telling stories of their shared past.

"I'm beginning to wonder if this isn't some kind of—" Sue never had a chance to finish her words.

"There," Brad said.

Through the empty windows that may have once been filled with elaborate stained glass there was a muted glow, like a light seen from miles away. Gradually, over a period of five minutes, it seemed to coalesce into a brighter light. For a long time it just hovered in one place, but eventually it began to drift slowly in one direction and then another.

"You two stay out here. I want to have another look inside," said Brad. He pushed the gate open, its creaking as loud as a scream this time.

Nothing had changed inside the old church since their earlier visit. The floorboards creaked under the pressure of his boots. Slowly he walked around the sanctuary, his eyes scanning the darkness for some sign he wasn't alone.

After his search, Brad came outside and leaned against the car. "I couldn't see a thing in there."

"What about the light?" asked Sue.

"Dear, there was no light inside. I wish there had been. I darn near broke my neck when I tripped over one of the pews," he said.

"Now this is getting weird," Sue said.

Brad felt a cold shiver run up his spine. "What do you mean?"

"From out here, we could still see the light, even after you went inside," said Steve. "It seemed to be hovering over

ou, moving whenever you did, and following you all over
1e sanctuary.''

Brad turned around toward the church. He could see the
.ght; it was still there.

"I think we've seen enough of this for tonight," said Sue.
'Why don't we head back into town?''

Neither her husband nor his friend objected to the sugges-
.on.

As their car pulled away, the glow inside the old building
egan to gently pulse, like the rhythm of someone's breath-
1g.

The abandoned church is approximately three to four miles
ast of Lawton. Take the Old Cache Road toward the town
f Cache; the church will be on the right-hand side of the
oad.

# Foster's Vanishing Farmhouse

I t was on an evening in May 1972 when the moon was full Six high school students were cruising around the back roads of Rhode Island in a beat-up old car, looking for a place to party.

These weren't rowdy kids, nor were they looking for trou ble. They wanted to smoke and drink beer—even have some intense conversations—and they were looking for an isolated quiet place to have fun because they didn't want to bother anyone. In fact, they were the "artsy" types from the local high school—serious students, members of the choir and the drama club.

They had driven out from the center of Chepachet, Rhode Island, going west on Route 102. The kids were still within the town limits when they spotted a small dirt road hedged in by trees. They hadn't noticed this road before and though they'd found the perfect place for a party. But when they'd driven down the road for about half a mile from the highway they discovered they were not driving on a road at all, bu a driveway. And ahead of them was a house in obvious disrepair.

In the light of the full moon, they could see an old two-story house, a barn, and a garage. There was also a neglected apple orchard. This was obviously an abandoned farm-house—or so they thought until they went inside.

The six students trooped into the house to investigate—the doors were not locked—and were surprised at what they found. Unused and dusty dishes, cups, pots and pans were stacked neatly on shelves in the kitchen. Silverware was tar-nishing slowly in the drawers. The curtains, though rotting, still hung from the windows. Moldy carpets covered the floors.

In the parlor, opposite the fireplace, an upright piano stood forgotten against the wall. All the furniture was in place, though dusty and moldering.

The kids went up to the second floor and found the upstairs bedrooms were the same way. All the furniture was intact. Tattered clothing hung in the closets. Beds were neatly made, though dingy. The bureaus were full.

Further investigation of the rest of the second floor was not possible. The floorboards were rotted with age and looked as though they might collapse at any moment. Decid-ing the house was too strange to stay in, the kids went down-stairs; they would have their party, but perhaps the yard was safer.

The six friends passed through the kitchen on their way out. One girl called their attention to a picture calendar hang-ing from a nail by the kitchen door. It was dated May 1946.

Outside, the kids looked at the other buildings. In the garage, two cars sat gathering rust. One sat on flat, rotting tires; the other was up on blocks, its wheels removed, its hood missing, tools and parts scattered about.

The barn was full of tools: rakes, pitchforks, scythes, assorted hand tools, and some agricultural implements, but no tractor to pull them. The barn had two stalls with troughs, but there were no signs of animals, ghostly or otherwise.

The house, though empty and abandoned, was completely intact. It looked as if one day the family who lived there had simply gotten up and walked out, never to return. And, according to the calendar, it happened almost twenty-six years ago to the day.

The kids finally gathered under one of the apple trees, and their partying was exceptionally quiet that night. And though they consumed beer and smoked pot, nobody got drunk or stoned. They were too affected by the aura of the abandoned farm. Instead of carousing, they speculated about what might have happened to the family who once lived there. The friends were determined to come back and investigate the house in daylight.

But high school kids being what they are, they didn't make it back the next day. But a few days later one of them drove down Route 102. He was surprised to find that fence posts and a chained gate suddenly had appeared, blocking the entrance to the dirt road.

The students decided that the gate and chain would not keep them away from the old farmhouse. The following week they piled into the car and drove down the highway. But though each of them knew the area well and there were clear landmarks along Route 102, they could not find the entrance to the farmhouse. There was no sign of the reported chain and gate, absolutely no sign of a dirt road anywhere. The abandoned farmhouse had vanished as mysteriously as it had appeared.

Perhaps the teenagers had stumbled upon the farmhouse

because of just the right combination of time and place. It may be possible to find that house again, if the conditions are right. On some moonlit night in May, when you drive west of Chepachet, you might spot that dirt road and end up in the Dark Zone.

# LOCATION INDEX

Outside the United States

In the United States

"Subterranean Spirits," Pueblo, Colorado

"The Last Guest of the Home Comfort Hotel," St. Elmo, Colorado

"The Unfriendly House on Old Homestead Road," St. Charles, Illinois

"The Guardian Angel of Justice," Justice, Illinois

"Stay Out of Room 310," Columbia, Missouri

"The Spirit of the Organ Loft," Kansas City, Missouri

"The Lavender Lady of Lemp House," St. Louis, Missouri

"Mystery Hill," North Salem, New Hampshire

"The Case of the Jealous Ghost," Gilford, New Hampshire

"The Parkway Phantom," Toms River, New Jersey

"There Are More Than Spies at Spy House," Port Monmouth, New Jersey

"The Sweet Sixteen Specter," Antioch, New York

"My Name Is Dr. Z," Babylon and West Islip, New York

"The Williamsburg Wraith," Brooklyn, New York

"The Spirit Express," Chatham, New York

"Elementals, My Dear Watson," Kinderhook, New York

"The Headless Horseman," Kinderhook, New York

"Spectral Restorations," Nyack, New York

"Mrs. Ackley's Ghosts," Nyack, New York

"The Show Must Go On," Broken Arrow, Oklahoma

"Lawton's Elusive Light," Lawton, Oklahoma

"The Werewolf of Lawton," Lawton, Oklahoma

"Tulsa's Trick or Treat," Tulsa, Oklahoma

"Foster's Vanishing Farmhouse," Foster, Rhode Island

"The Greenville Ghost," Greenville, Rhode Island
"The Talking Cat of Danville," Danville, Virginia
"Bigfoot Central," Bothell, Duvall, Woodinville,
  Mt. Ranier National Park, Washington
"Juddville Is a State of Mind," Juddville,
  Wisconsin
"The Lloyd Street Gnome," Wauwatosa,
  Wisconsin

# EXPLORE THE DEADLY, *DOCUMENTED* DWELLINGS OF THE SUPERNATURAL!

Here are two unique guidebooks that provide a virtual travelogue to eerie locales around the world—places where people have experienced hauntings, evil forces, demons, spectral visitations, and poltergeists.

"Horrifying...awesome...a fascinating compilation...These places are real—so when you visit them, be careful!"

—John Keel, author of *Our Haunted Planet*

☐ **DEAD ZONES**
(F6-077, $4.50, USA)($5.99, Can.)

☐ **DARK ZONES**
(F36-078, $4.99, USA)($5.99, Can.)

**Warner Books P.O. Box 690
New York, NY 10019**

Please send me the books I have checked. I enclose a check or money order (not cash), plus 95¢ per order and 95¢ per copy to cover postage and handling,* or bill my ☐ American Express ☐ VISA ☐ MasterCard. (Allow 4-6 weeks for delivery.)

___Please send me your free mail order catalog. (If ordering only the catalog, include a large self-addressed, stamped envelope.)

Card # _____

Signature _____ Exp. Date _____

Name _____

Address _____

City _____ State _____ Zip _____
*New York and California residents add applicable sales tax.                    592